MW01127429

MOUNT OUTLOOK RAILWAY
MT. OR
OUTLOOK SPRINGS

COMPANY DIRECTORY

Outlook Springs is published under the oversight of Langston Brumbletooth, Conductor Emeritus of the Mt. Outlook Railway Services LTD.

The issue you're currently looking at is Number 8 from Summer 2022. There's a very good chance that there have been seven other issues before this one and if you're cool (like, really, really cool) you'll hop right on your internets and buy those other issues so you can have all eight, which, when combined, create a sort of flimsy approximation of a train station.

To submit your wordwork, tell us we're super-rad, or volunteer to explore the Endless Railways of Our Lord and Savior's Warped Curvature, use one and/or all of the following e-methods:

 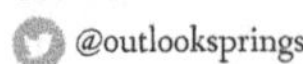  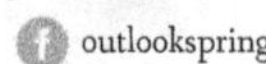

PASSENGER MANIFEST

CONSTANCE BACCHUS

MATTHEW CHAMBERLIN

FRANKLIN K.R. CLINE

MARISA CRANE

SHAWN DELGADO

ZAKIYYAH DZUKOGI

DANIEL GALEF

BERNADETTE GEYER

GARY GLASS

ROBIN GOW

SORAMIMI HANAREJIMA

GRETA HAYER

REBECCA HIGGINS

CLAIRE HOPPLE

SATOSHI IWAI

CASEY MCCONAHAY

LAURA MCGEHEE

LINCOLN MICHEL

KYLE E MILLER

MICHAEL P. MORAN

MARY LYNN REED

XAVIER REYNA

JOHN RIEBOW

MICHELLE ROSS

TOM ROTH

RAE ROZMAN

BILLY THRASHER

SAMUEL ZAGULA

TABLE OF CONTENTS

TAB-O-CON, PART TWO

PRE-HISTORY

Coal bunker

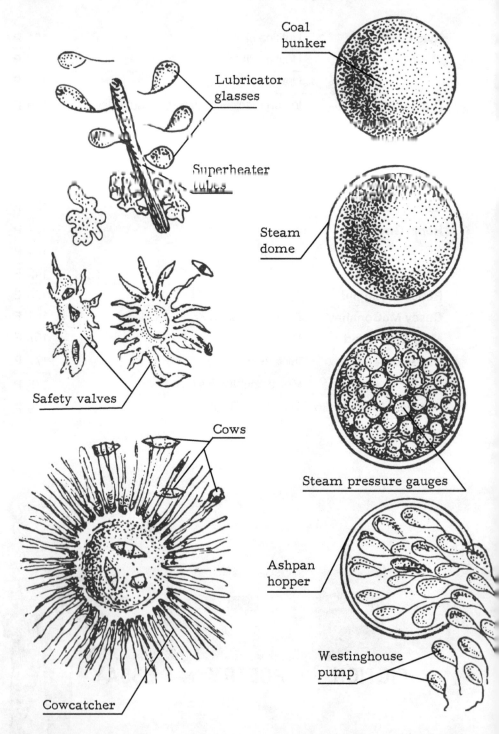

Lubricator glasses

Superheater tubes

Steam dome

Safety valves

Cows

Steam pressure gauges

Ashpan hopper

Westinghouse pump

Cowcatcher

OUR HISTORY

Established in the latter half of Epoch 12.c by Greg, The Mt. Outlook Railway, which may be better known as "Old Oaty," is the first free particle, Space/Time-climbing railway in the multiverse. It is considered one of the Top 12 "Marvels of Quantum Engineering" by Choo-Choo Magazine, and was voted "Fourth Best Mobile Eggs Benedict in the Triangulum Galaxy" for 207 past, present, and future eons.

To ride Old Oaty is to be transported into an unforgettable, unrememberable era of superpositional luxury, which is why it has continued to enchant passengers from all over the worlds: from Sandpoint, Idaho all the way to the Devil's Singularity. Feel the gentle rumble and rattle of our original fog-powered locusmotive as it chugs along the copper-and-oak electroad 3.7 lightyears per lightyear. Look out our award-winning windows and gaze upon the starry fields of forever, each twist and turn revealing a new stunning vista of infinity. You may even catch a glimpse of local wildflife: a moose or...an even bigger moose. Feeling sleepy? Slip into our CryoCart® ("Cryopreservation You Can Depend On, Mostly") and enjoy the gentle pleasures of deep epochal emptiness. When you thaw, come on down Planck's Constant Pub for an ice-cold Hydrogen-and-Tonic or an Entanglemint Julip, or spoil yourself with a steamy dreamy plate of our legendary Paradox a l'Orange smothered (or not!) in homemade Schrödinger's-style catsup.

SO DON'T BE A PHLOGISTON! PURCHASE YOUR TICKETS TODAY: §29.95 APIECE. BRING THE FAMILY. THERE'S NO TIME LIKE THE PRESENT. IN FACT, THERE'S NO TIME AT ALL.

TICKETS & MAP

ADULT . . . . §29^{95}
CHILD. . . . . §39^{95}
ELDER . . . . §19^{95}
ANCIENT ONE . . . . §█
GROUP (4+). . . . . §19^{95} ea.
HORDE. . . . . §58 ea.
GASEOUS/LIQUID/ENERGY . . . . §80
THEORETICAL. . . . . §$(N \times A^{\mu})$
GREG OR GREG-ADJACENT. . . . . §GREG^{99}
SPACE-COLLIE (W/ NECESSARY SHOTS) . . . . . . §149^{95}
FROG (W/ OR W/O NECESSARY SHOTS) . . . . §139^{95}

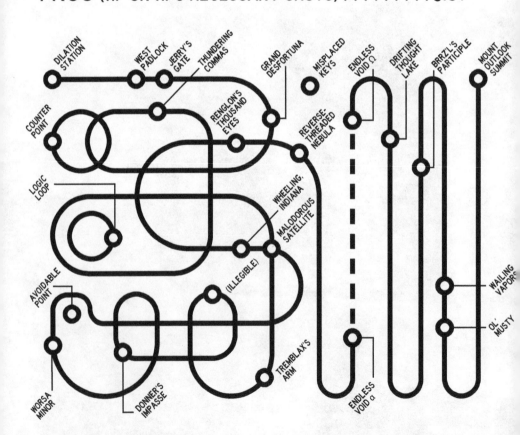

DILATION STATION
WEST PADLOCK
JERRY'S GATE
THUNDERING COMMAS
GRAND DESFORTUNA
MISPLACED KEYS
ENDLESS VOID Ω
DRIFTING THOUGHT LAKE
BRRZ'L'S PARTICIPLE
MOUNT OUTLOOK SUMMIT
COUNTER POINT
RENGLON'S THOUSAND EYES
REVERSE-THREADED NEBULA
LOGIC LOOP
WHEELING, INDIANA
MALODOROUS SATELLITE
AVOIDABLE POINT
(ILLEGIBLE)
WAILING VAPORS
OL' MUSTY
TREMBLAX'S ARM
WORSA MINOR
DONNER'S IMPASSE
ENDLESS VOID α

CLAIRE HOPPLE

FEED US TO THE SWANS

BECAUSE NOW THEY ARE BEING INTERROGATED, five hours after breaking and entering, six hours after deciding to break-and-enter, and one day after receiving an eviction notice, all she wants to do is tell the truth.

She trespasses. She does so whenever she can.

It doesn't take long for a froth of confession to cultivate in her throat, lashing her organs and xylophoning her ribs.

The thing that concerns her the most: how willing she is to talk. How unfazed she can be. And just how navigable the situation appears.

"This car was creeping down the road, going 29 right in front of me. I wanted to tail him but then I saw all the memorial decals along the back windshield dedicated to some relative. I thought, maybe I shouldn't; maybe he's in mourning. And then I thought, well, he had time to get those decals made, how fresh could it be? And then I thought, when *isn't* he in mourning though? And then I thought, when aren't we *all* in mourning? So I applied pressure to the gas pedal."

Her accomplice is stalling. The officers are blinking at him.

"Look, we have plenty more tangents where that came from," she adds.

Rampant notions are their specialty.

"And while I'm on the subject—" he attempts to cut back in.

"—It was simple. We broke in," she says. "At the rate we were going, we'd cover our debts in, I don't know, two or three lifetimes."

He was supposed to preside over the porch when they arrived but he became less of a guard and more of a Walmart greeter when neighbors started walking their dogs up and down the street.

Meanwhile, she was concocting a path to imagined treasure troves deposited throughout the house. But on her way through, the old lady announced herself.

"I've been expecting you," Mrs. Anderson said.

"What do you mean? How did you know?" she asked.

"That's what the others asked me too," Mrs. Anderson said.

She didn't want to assume but Mrs. Anderson didn't elaborate so she did anyway. It's probably because Mrs. Anderson owns this town. Like, she literally bought it. If she were Mrs. Anderson, she'd reasonably surmise that you don't leave a property like this and expect it to be there when you get back. In fact, Mrs. Anderson hadn't even left and here they were establishing themselves where they didn't belong.

"This place is basically a museum now," Mrs. Anderson sighed. "Still, these Milano cookies were half price this morning, and that's something. Can you believe it?"

She feigned a customary facial expression in response.

Back at the station, her partner says, "After we had given up, right when we thought she'd feed us to her swans, she offered us the pact."

"Mrs. Anderson looks right at him and admits that she is his secret admirer," she says.

He's been receiving unspeakable letters, crafts, shrines, artfully positioned roadkill—the works—on his front stoop for years.

"But Mrs. Anderson doesn't stop there," she says. "Then, she tells us that 'according to vague calculations' she is a fortune teller, but only while she sleeps. I asked her if she ever tried to detect these abilities when fully awake and she said it was against her principles."

"Are you getting this down?" he asks one of the officers, who shifts in his seat.

"So I bet you're wondering about the pact. What it was and how it transpired. Basically, she agreed to tell our fortunes if we obliged her by tucking her in bed with some tea and a record full of plucked harp strings. And, of course, not pilfering any of her valuables. To seal the deal, she embroiders the scene of our pact—albeit a rather primitive rendering—of the three of us hovering around her coffee table. Mrs. Anderson's pretty quick with a needle and thread," she continues.

That had really put a cap on the day. Mrs. Anderson had neglected to tell them that she snores her way through fortune telling, making crucial testaments a challenge to decipher. But they were able to get the gist.

Mrs. Anderson told the woman that one day she'd be sitting on a bench that was dedicated to herself, with a little plaque and everything. She told the man that he would die soon, but that "a funeral is the highest form of marketing."

Now he says to the cops, "None of that matters to me."

"And I guess somewhere along the way, nobody'd stopped her from picking up the phone and calling you guys, though I don't really see how we missed that," she says to the tirelessly tired officers in front of her.

At least the very last thing Mrs. Anderson ever told her, she keeps to herself. She said to the woman, "How much of knowing your future changes what you're doing?" And then, "Oh, your escorts have arrived."

DIRECTIONS, PART ONE

LOCATED IN THE WARPED CURVATURE OF THE MASSIVE OUTLOOK MOUNTAINS, MT. OUTLOOK RAIL DEPARTS AN INFINITE NUMBER OF TIMES, SIMULTANEOUSLY, FROM DILATION STATION. GLOBAL POSITIONING SYSTEM (GPS) ACCESS IS EXTREMELY LIMITED, SO IT'S CRUCIAL YOU FOLLOW THE BELOW DIRECTIONS CLOSELY.

FROM SANDPOINT, IDAHO:

Head North on N. Fifth Avenue toward Cedar Street (.02 m)

Turn left onto Church Street (375 ft)

Keep right at the fork (1.2 m)

Keep left of the spoon (.05 m)

Merge onto US-95 (6.5 m)

Take exit toward ID-53 W (UNKNOWN)

Take a left at the big berry bush and drive through the portal of heatshimmer (.08 m)

SCREAM AS LOUD AS YOU CAN (400 ft)

L O U D E R (20 ft.)

DON'T BLINK (18.6 m)

At the traffic circle, keep circling at a high speed/low velocity (∞)

At the traffic dodecahedron, astral project bilaterally along the magellanic filament (varies depending on make of vehicle)

DIRECTIONS, PART TWO

Wrong filament, but we can make this work via lunar occultation electro-vaporation (1.7 dv)

While we're here, let's stop for a Big Bang Mac at CosMicdonald's (look for Golden Archimedes) (.00006 units)

It's closed for Spherical Geometry Appreciation Week? Are Euclidding me? (let's just go by instinct, yeah?)

TURN ON THE RADIO (power button)

Wait, stop. Listen. This is that song I was telling you about earlier. The song about the guy... the guy with the broken heart... and now he's lonely. Come on, you know the one I'm talking about, right? (33 m/s)

Take exit 55 onto Pleasant Avenue (.05 m)

That's not a cop. No. Those aren't lights. That's a ski rack. (55.6 deep breaths)

Take right and another quick right at OUTLOOK STATE PARK (16 otterlengths)

Park at Dilation Station. Right there next to the crimson sedan. (4 spots over)

Did you even know it was Spherical Geometry Appreciation Week? I feel like it kind of snuck up on us this year (...)

YOU HAVE ARRIVED AT YOUR DESTINATION.

FROM ANYWHERE ELSE:

RUN INTO THE RAIN

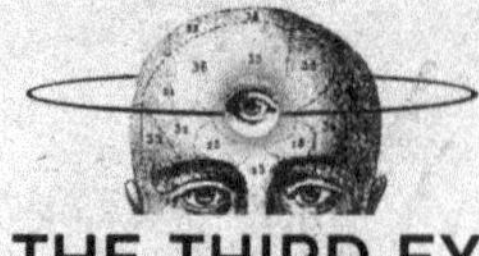

In the movie "Communion" when the three arrow-triangles of the clock line up, the aliens come. After his "experience" he sees normal people as insectoid "alien" drones. Time 1:11.

III THE THIRD EYE

[illegible] The alien experience happens externally, the message is the same as the one processed internally?

***BRIGHT LIGHTS *ESP**

Ego Dissolution? ***QBL}-ABYSS}-BREAKDOWN OF FORCES}-RECYCLES**

***THE CHOSEN *DREAMLIKE**

**multiple layers of mirrors hiding true forms*

THE SOTHIC CYCLE IS THE PERIOD OF RETURN OF THE HELIACAL RISING OF SIRIUS WHICH IS 365.25 DAYS, RISING AT DAWN JUST AHEAD OF THE SUN IN THE EASTERN PORTION OF THE SKY, THE ONLY STAR TO DO SO.

"I've seen my whole life and they compiled it and now it's passed on to my son."

You saw something extraordinary, you saw God, God has many faces, You come back, youre different, They given you a gift. Youd better use it.

research time speed of travel from Sirius to Earth 1972-1985-2002

"The Black Rite is the Secret of Secrets and even those who know it do not know it fully; but it will be revealed when we pursue Isis and Osiris unto the heights, yea, into the starry infinity."

SHAWN DELGADO

DO NOT FEED THE ANIMALS [I]

Because they look hungry

Even if you think you spot
its skull pressing
through a patch
beside the gray eye.

Because you are amused

To see them beg
and roll or leap
and slobber. Never sated
in their stupid joy.

Because they might love you

Forgetting their instincts
and their gods,
they might come back
hungry and with knowledge.

POETRY

SHAWN DELGADO

DO NOT FEED THE ANIMALS [II]

It is not natural.
Their migrations are delicate,
Their habitats, moreso.

You are disrupting their grazing habits.
Your bread is poison inside them
Our food is scarce.

They will forget to hunt.
They are an invasive species.
It ruins the instincts of the young.

Their bellies are never satisfied.
They might love you.
They don't know when to stop.

There will be a plague if their prey go unchecked.
They will abandon their gods.
They will not leave. They will return.

SHAWN DELGADO

WE DO NOT MAKE DOILIES UPON WHICH A DELICATE TEACUP MAY REST BREATHING STEAM

We build tables
you can stand on
jump on
that an entire family
can stomp on
five generations
thirty-one cousins at least invited
and most turn up
for the dance
to celebrate your wedding
where you all leap at once

We build houses
that stand in magnitude eight
earthquakes or tornadoes
where the ripping wind
is a hot knife
in snow
but even when a Holstein heifer
and a baby grand piano slam the roof
you don't lose a shingle
and the cow somehow lives
and learns to play Chopin

Our instruments are not gentle
murmurs the shade of sunset
they oomp and awk
coat the air in coloratura
or crack drums like Brazil nuts
in a giant crab's claw

never softly, the piano,
except when the glissando
reduces each listener
to the size of a fly
who can now hear
every note in his beard

BILLY THRASHER

THE FIGHT FOR NORMALCY

Randy Siems was only thirteen years old but had had enough. "I'm gonna' try and blow my lungs up." Not only did his skinny five-foot eight-inch frame weigh a mere one hundred twenty-five pounds, but it also had what Randy called a crater in the middle of his chest. So, he went downstairs, grabbed two dumbbells, and leaned back onto his fathers' work bench, intent on using the butterfly exercise to blow up his lungs. At this time, Randy did not know that the cause of this deformity was *Pectus Excavatum*.

According to Pectus.com, *Pectus Excavatum* is the most common congenital deformity of the anterior wall of the chest in which several ribs and the sternum grow abnormally. This produces a caved-in or sunken appearance. It can be present at birth or may not develop until puberty, as was the case for Randy. Up to the age of thirteen, Randy loved to ride his bike and swim, but when he entered puberty the crater in his chest become noticeable.

Randy said, "It was so extreme that if I had a shirt on, and the wind blew, it would just blow right into the crater."

Not only was his chest a cause of anxiety, but Randy's earliest recollection goes back to kindergarten when he received weekly shots of epinephrine to combat his asthma and took a daily prescription medicine to alleviate his allergies. Though Randy was a sickly child, he was also active with what we now call Attention Deficit Disorder. This combination of health ailments kept him in what Randy considered a constant struggle for normalcy.

As he sat in the basement on the workbench and took a gigantic breath and spread his arms outward into the butterfly position, he said to himself, "If my chest pops like a balloon, I'll just fall over there. I just don't care. I don't care." Randy brought his arms together above his chest. It didn't pop. He did it over and over again, and still nothing popped. He did twenty more repetitions, and still nothing happened.

Finally, Randy put the weights down and stood up. The first thing he noticed was that he could breathe a lot better. He was so excited that he ran upstairs and told his mom, but she told him to stop because the doctor said the extra activity would aggravate his asthma. She also said, "I'm gonna tell your father." But filled with this new discovery, Randy said, "I don't care if you tell him. I'm doing it again." So he went downstairs and finished his workout. This was the beginning of what would become his lifestyle.

By the time Randy was fifteen, he had committed to a seven-day workout routine—two hours each day devoted to lifting weights and cardiovascular exercises—which kept his asthma under control. The allergies were also controlled because he had completely changed his eating habits, eating food primarily from the Shaklee food and supplement company. This was very expensive for his parents. At this point, Randy said, "I beat the asthma. I beat the allergies. Now I'm gonna get rid of this crater in my chest because this thing is ruining me."

Randy was at a friend's house when he saw a picture of Arnold Schwarzenegger. Randy said, "I want to be like that. You know why? Because Arnold doesn't have a crater in his chest."

Arnold Schwarzenegger had yet to star in his breakthrough film "Conan the Barbarian" but had won the "Mr. Universe" competition as an amateur (once) and as a pro (three times) as well as the title of Mr. Olympia. The poster displayed Schwarzenegger's classic pose: left arm bent, hand behind his head showing his tri-cep, right arm horizontal and flexed to show his bicep, and ripped abs that funneled up from his trimmed waist. But Randy was focused on the two pectoral muscles on each side of his chest that measured 57 inches in circumference and allowed him to bench press more than 500 pounds.

Randy's incentive was to lift enough weights to make, as he put it, "big fat muscles" to fill up the crater in his chest. By age fifteen, he had grown to about five-feet-ten inches and weighed one-hundred-fifty pounds. For the next two years, with the help of a friend who worked at the appropriately named New Life Fitness Center, Randy was able to access more advanced weight machines. After two years, Randy had grown another inch but only gained twenty pounds. His arms, chest, and shoulders were getting bigger, and he thought he was going to correct his deformity. So he committed to his routine up to the age of twenty one and gained another twenty pounds of muscle. But after all his work, the crater was still there.

At his point, the deformity was taking a serious chunk out of his social life. Wind was pushing his shirt into the crater, making the impression of an empty bowl. He never went to a public swimming pool. Randy had yet to have a long-term relationship, and any time he had a chance of becoming intimate with a girl the lights had to be turned off.

The next step was steroids. He wanted bigger muscles, not for strength but to fill the crater in his chest. The steroids worked on his muscles. Randy went from one-hundred-ninety pounds to two-hundred-fifteen pounds in only four months. Though he got bigger muscles, the crater was still there.

For those diagnosed with *Pectus Excavatum*, many scales have been developed to determine the degree of deformity in the chest wall. The Haller index is measured by forming a ratio of the distance of the inside of the ribcage and the shortest distance between the vertebrae and sternum. A normal chest index is 2.5, and an index over 3.25 is defined as severe. Randy's Haller index was measured at 4.6.

Randy was furious. He read an interview in which Arnold Schwarzenegger said that pullovers were the best way to expand the rib cage. Randy thought this was the answer for sure, so he "did more pullovers than anyone in the state of Missouri," he recalled. By the time Randy was twenty-five years old, he was six-feet tall and weighed two-hundred-twenty pounds. But his chest still had the crater.

He had been fighting this deformity for more than ten years and had not won. He only knew he had to work harder.

The deformity was in control of all his decisions. Not only from a physical point of view but from a mental perspective as well. He was determined to hide his deformity from everyone, so he came up with excuses to avoid any activities that involved showing his chest and began to fill all of his time with work.

Three principles governed his life: work harder in the gym, work harder at his business, and above all, become an overachiever at everything he was involved in. Randy thought he had it covered. He spent many hours as a salesman for his construction company, working ten to twelve hour days, six to seven days a week. His company grew, and when he sensed the market begin to slow, he sold the company at the age of thirty-five. Then he entered the real estate business, buying and rehabbing houses and keeping some as rental homes. He spent all his free time in the gym, and he wanted to be the best he could be to show people that he was just like them.

Randy's mental obsession with his deformity was not unusual. According to Pectus.com, *Pectus Excavatum* often plays a major factor in all decisions made by those born with it. Even after having the correction performed, former patients often don't participate in anything that will reveal their chest. The physical deformity can be corrected, but the mental struggle never leaves them.

Randy continued to "work, work, work" with little to no social life until he was forty-three years old and still hiding his deformity. At this time, he was exercising at Gold's Gym in Creve Coeur every day of the week but no longer taking steroids, though he had switched to an over-the-counter supplement to take their place.

One evening, while working out, he loaded the straight bar with three hundred and sixty-five pounds, his usual routine. As he pushed the bar above his chest, he heard a pop so loud it sounded like a car crash. He lay there in shock, and soon realized that his pectoral muscle had torn away from his clavicle and was sagging at his rib cage. He was taken to the emergency room at DePaul Health Center but could not get surgery at that time because it was discovered that he had Atrial Fibrillation, an irregular heartbeat, which requires a special sedative for surgery.

Eventually, his pectoral muscle was repaired, but the Atrial Fibrillation caught Randy's attention. After doing some research, he found that it could be related to *Pectus Excavatum*. After thirty years of dodging social situations to hide his chest and lifting weights to fight his deformity, finally, because of a freak accident, he had discovered the origin of his constant torment. Yet Randy did not dwell on the past, because now he knew exactly what he was fighting.

He began to post in a forum on the pectusinfo.com website, along with other people dealing with the same deformity. Eventually, he communicated with Steve Chen, a doctor in Hollywood, California, who was a specialist in the *Pectus Excavatum* surgery. By this time in Randy's life, overachieving tendencies had become so engrained that he expected the same from anyone else, especially a doctor who was going to operate on his chest. Before hiring a doctor, Randy's requirement was that the doctor had performed a minimum of 250 operations.

At this time, three primary methods were used to repair *Pectus Excavatum*: the Leonard, Nuss, and Ravitch procedures, or a combination of Nuss/Ravitch.

The Ravitch procedure is invasive and involves cutting away the rib cartilages and flattening the sternum. One or more bars (or struts) may then be inserted to ensure the sternum keeps its shape. The bars are left in place until the cartilage grows back, usually about six months, and then removed during a simple out-patient surgery. This procedure is not widely used because it is considered invasive due to the incision into the skin and removal of cartilage.

The Nuss procedure, developed by Dr. Donald Nuss, is widely used because it is minimally invasive. Two or three incisions are made on each side of the chest, depending on how many bars the patient is going to receive. The bars are inserted through the incisions and under the sternum. The bar is then flipped, and the sternum pops out. A stabilizer plate is also inserted around the bar and the rib cage in order to support the bars and keep them in place. After a period of two to four years, the bars are removed from the patient chest during out-patient surgery.

Randy requested the Nuss procedure to correct his *Pectus Excavatum.*

He wanted an expert in the field of *Pectus Excavatum*; Dr. Chen had only performed six operations. Regardless of the number of surgeries that Randy wanted his surgeon to have performed, most of the doctors he contacted would not perform the surgery because he was an adult. At this time in America, the *Pectus Excavatum* correction was only performed on children and adolescents.

Randy's search continued until he found Dr. Klaus Schaarschmidt, or Dr. Schar, whose practice was located in Berlin, Germany.

Randy contacted Dr. Schar, and the first thing he said to Randy was, "I've been waiting for your call." The doctor had been reading the forum at the Pectusinfo website and knew about Randy. After thirty years of waging war against himself, he was finally talking to the man who could help him correct this deformity.

On November 20, 2007, at the age of forty-five, Randy flew to Berlin, Germany to correct what had plagued him for more than thirty years. Though Dr. Schar had performed this procedure on all ages, at this time Randy was the oldest adult in the world to have this procedure completed.

Today, *Pectus Excavatum* is detected early in life and corrected regularly in children and adolescents before they reach adulthood. The procedure is similar to getting braces, in that after a certain amount of time—after the bones have been reformed to a normal condition—the bars are removed.

Still, many patients who have had the correction still won't go out in public with their shirt off or participate in activities they think will reveal the deformity they used to have.

Randy never accepted that he was going to be "a sick kid, sitting on a couch." His parents always told him it was no big deal and to ignore it, but *Pectus Excavatum* is a physical and mental deformity that had factored into every part of his life.

Now in his mid-fifties, Randy is more social than before the operation and doesn't really mind people who see him without a shirt, though he has kept the same overachieving work ethic since he first began his journey. He has thought about getting the bars removed, but unless they become a health issue, they will remain in his chest.

Sources:
Randy Seims
Pectus.com

Sources no longer available:
Pectusinfo.com
Pectus.org

EMPLOYMENT OPPORTUNITIES

CO-DIRECTOR OF DEAGITATION & UNMISALIGNMENT

Have you ever wanted to spend your days realigning misaligned expectoratory mechanisms and reorganzing disorganized fenestration occlusions? Apply now to become an unseparate aspect of the consciousness collective responsible for recalibrating the countless ejectional and mechano-optical systems that sustain Old Oaty and live out the dreams of you and the eternal others.

EVAPORATION, DEMARCATION & CONSECRATION INTERN

Learn the thrills of overseeing perspiratory bladders and tubes, the excitement of indicating the limits of specified items within a known or unknown set, and the supreme satisfaction of having the motions of the necessary rites to maintain complex systems drilled into your mind so that you can perform them (the rites) in your sleep! Achieve great renown in small circles of coworkers, strain your psyche to its absolute limit and beyond, and never worry about the encumbrance of wealth, or even sufficient earnings! Concluding reading this sentence signifies your acceptance of all internship terms and waiving of all necessary rights so as to be able to perform your new duties. Welcome to your eternal internship, we'll see you bright and early on Monday! Bring lunch.

TERTIARY PRINCIPAL IN CHARGE OF ELECTRO-, PHOTO-, & ORGANO-SYNTHESIS

If you have experience coördinating multiple synthesis systems utilizing various operating languages, then we just might have the opportunity of multiple lifetimes for you, and the energy that animates your corporeal being. Apply now!

PHOSPHORESCENCE EXECUTIVE OFFICER, NTH CLASS

Are you a bright go-getter with a glowing résumé, willing to bring endless energy to a vibrant community of radiant organisms, all working in unison to illuminate the hidden bowels of an interdimensional train? Then we have the position for you! Apply to be a member of our valuable internal illumination department now!

SPATIAL, DIMENSIONAL & CHRONOLOGICAL MULTIPLICITY MANIPULATION & INTEGRATION LIEUTENANT

Are you a conglomeration of numerous self-aware entities capable of integrating into many varied realities simultaneously? Do you have at least 1×10^9 æons of experience? Apply now!

FROG, NOT DEAD

We need a new frog for the frogshow.

LINCOLN MICHEL

HANSEL AND GRETEL'S TEETH

Hansel and Gretel never fully recovered from the gingerbread house. Yes, there was the psychological trauma of their imprisonment and torture, but there were also their teeth. For weeks, they'd been force-fed gumdrops and marshmallows without ever being allowed to brush. Although their late father had been but a poor woodcutter, he'd always stressed the importance of dental hygiene. The witch hadn't cared. She'd been planning to eat almost everything except the teeth. Now, their mouths were full of cavities and their tongues swam in swamps of pus and blood.

Hansel and Gretel decided to go to the dentist.

What the receptionist said made Gretel shriek.

"I'm sorry," the woman said. "That's our cheapest option. We aren't tooth fairies. We have a business to run here."

"But we have health insurance!" Hansel said.

"That only covers your body, not your teeth," the receptionist said. There was a bowl of lollipops in front of her. The receptionist unwrapped a green one and sucked.

"My teeth are part of my body. See?" Gretel pointed a finger at her inflamed gums.

"Not for the purposes of medical coverage." The receptionist handed the siblings a couple brochures. "I'd also recommend vision insurance. You can never be too careful with your eyes and teeth. You've only got one set of each."

Hansel and Gretel were broke. Their father had injured himself chopping wood and the hospital bills had gobbled up all the pearls they'd smuggled from the witch's gingerbread house as easily as a bird pecking breadcrumbs from the forest floor.

Hansel and Gretel walked out of the dentist's office, blood in their mouths.

"Bunch of crooks," Hansel said.

"Highway robbery," Gretel mumbled.

But it was the same at the second dentist office and also at the third. Every dentist in the village wanted to charge exorbitant fees that were multiplied by the large number of diseased teeth.

The siblings went to a local apothecary and spent their last coins on herbal teas and twig brushes. Nothing worked. They stopped chewing food and ate only mush and soup. At night, Hansel moaned either in pain or in memory of his time in the witch's cage while Gretel rubbed his head and said, "there, there."

One day, their rabbit trap caught something strange. A small goblin with perfect white teeth.

"Where did you get those pearly whites?" Gretel demanded.

The goblin trembled in the wooden rabbit trap. "I'm not allowed to say."

"Then we'll have to eat you up," Hansel said, although his jaw ached at the thought of chewing notoriously tough goblin flesh.

Hansel raised his father's ax.

"Okay! Okay! You got me," the goblin said. "I can lead you to a magical dentist who can fix any mouth."

"Where?" Gretel asked.

"Her house is deep in the forest. I'll show you, I promise."

The siblings withdrew behind a tangled bush to discuss. They were both hesitant to trust a goblin—and a green one at that!—and they remembered what happened last time they went strolling through the deep dark woods. But what choice did they have? So they made a deal with the goblin, whose name was Gunther.

Gretel went back to their house and grabbed a handful of pebbles from the driveway. They were as white and sharp as teeth. She wouldn't make the mistake of breadcrumbs again! The three went off into the black forest. Hansel held his father's ax and Gretel dropped a pebble every so often.

After a couple hours, Gunther started chattering his teeth in fear. "Oh no," he said through the clacking. "I'm going to ruin them already."

"What are you afraid of?" Gretel asked. Yet Gunther had already run off. The siblings watched his flailing green arms disappear into the forest.

It didn't matter. They could see their destination in a clearing ahead. It was a big white cottage in the shape of a single tooth.

When they got to the front yard, they realized the cottage was made of countless tiny teeth. Molars, incisors, and canines all stuck together with a gummy glue. The must have been thousands—no millions—of teeth.

"Let's go back," Hansel said, sensibly.

Gretel ran a jealous finger along a row of smooth wisdoms. Her own teeth throbbed with pain. "No one will help us in town, Hansel. This is our only chance to smile again."

The jawbone door opened and a witch came out wearing a long white coat. She had a mask over her mouth and a magical amulet on her forehead that shone in their eyes.

"Well, well. What have we here?"

Hansel and Gretel were so shocked they couldn't speak. Their mouths hung wide in fear.

The witch peered into their open mouths and examined their bleeding gums and rotting teeth.

"Haven't you children got a sweet tooth."

"It's not our fault!" Gretel protested.

"We weren't allowed to brush," Hansel said.

"No, matter, no matter. Let's strap you into the examination chair."

The children didn't move. They held each other's hands and hung their heads.

"We don't have any dental insurance," Hansel said.

The witch pulled down her facemask. She stared at them. Then she cackled. "I guess we'll just have to work out an alternate payment plan."

The witch yanked off a couple rows of tooth siding for the operation, then took Hansel and Gretel in the house. The inside was very clean but contained a strange smell. It seemed to be coming from the locked wooden door that led to the basement.

"Did something die down there?" Gretel said.

The witch sniffed with her hairy green schnoz. "Hmm, must be my dental supplies. I guess I'm just used to the smell."

There was a big wooden chair in the center of the room with leather straps. Hansel volunteered to go first while Gretel stood watch. The witch used a silver wand and metal pliers to yank out and replace all of Hansel's teeth. There was a lot of blood. Yet, after rinsing out his mouth, Hansel admired his beautiful new smile.

"Wow, they're so white and free of cracks," he said.

Gretel then got the yank, bleed, and replace treatment. They both danced across the molar floor and thanked the witch profusely.

"Good, good!" the witch said, grinning to show her own long teeth. "Now, let's talk payment."

And so Hansel and Gretel began their new life as assistants to the dentist witch. Although the witch called them hygienists, most of their time was spent procuring new teeth. "You can never have enough stock," the witch would say and send them to graveyard with a pair of spades and pliers.

The witch had calculated their debt at one thousand teeth each. Hansel protested—they'd only used 28 apiece after all—but the witch said this was standard markup plus time, labor, and overhead. The witch put magic collars on their necks that would cause them to howl in pain if they didn't meet their weekly quotas. "This is called an incentive," the witch said. The only other rules were that they had to brush the walls of teeth every week and they were forbidden to go into the dark basement.

The siblings worked for the witch for some time. They dug up graves until their hands were filled with splinters from the wooden handles of their spades. They knocked out teeth from skulls until the metal blades were filled with dings. And they ripped their clothes scrambling away as the police and priests ran into the graveyard to stop them.

A few times, to make their quota, Hansel had to pick fights with ruffians and aim for the jaw. Gretel would collect the teeth when they fell in the dirt.

But eventually there were no more teeth to pull out or pick up. They'd dug up all the graves in the surrounding towns and Hansel had been beat up so often that he'd lost half the teeth the witch had given him. They tried bringing the witch a bag of dog teeth, but she wasn't fooled.

"You'll have to live here as my servants now. Clean up the blood from the floor and feed me my breakfast in bed!"

When they tried to run away, their enchanted collars burned their necks. The siblings couldn't believe they'd been trapped again by yet another evil witch. Life was as rotten as their old teeth.

Then one day, when all the customers had gone home and the witch was snoring on her bed of nails, Gretel heard a sound.

She crept over and pressed her ear against the door that led to the basement.

"There's someone down there," she said.

Hansel trembled. He ran his tongue the between gaps in his teeth. "If we go down there, she'll add another hundred teeth to our bill!"

But Gretel had gotten sick of the witch and sick of working such a degrading job with no chance of advancement or escape. She took the black keychain out of the witch's coat pocket, which was hung on the back of the examination chair, and opened the basement door.

The siblings crept down the dark stairs with only a candle to light the way. The basement was dark and dusty. Rats and spiders scuttled away from their candlelight. The teeth that made up the walls and floor were yellow and moldy.

"Help," a small voice cried.

They saw a shivering creature with metallic wings chained to the wall.

"Hello," Gretel said. "I'm Gretel and this is Hansel. We're the dental hygienists. Why are you down here?"

The decrepit fairy looked up at them. "This is my house!" she cried.

"Your house?" Hansel said.

"Yes, my house! I'm a tooth fairy. I built this cottage out of all the teeth I collected from little boys and girls. Then the witch came and locked me in the basement and stole all my equipment and started selling the teeth I bought fair and square."

"She's evil!" Hansel said. "She makes us steal teeth from corpses to pay our dental bill."

"Let me free and I'll relieve you of your debt!" the fairy said.

Gretel scrambled over with the keys as quick as she could. They tried all the keys and finally the last one worked. The fairy flew with her metallic wings and grabbed a wand that was hanging on the wall from a pair of perpendicular front teeth. She cast two zaps at Hansel and Gretel and their enchanted necklaces fell on the floor.

The siblings laughed and hugged each other. Meanwhile, the fairy flew right up the steps and jabbed out the witch's eyes while she slept. A pained shriek filled the house. The fairy sliced off the witch's tongue and pulled off her ears with two big pops.

Hansel and Gretel ran upstairs to join the fun.

Gretel smacked the witch's teeth out of her mouth one by one with a spade. The witch screamed gurgles of blood. Hansel grabbed his father's ax and chopped the witch up from toes to head, as if she was one very long and very green sausage.

Together, the fairy, Gretel, and Hansel cleaned up the blood and agreed to go into business together.

"We'll be an ethical dentistry practice," Hansel said.

"We can charge fair rates and pay our employees enough that they never have to worry about going hungry or not affording needed medical procedures," Gretel added.

They got to work filling out the paperwork. Pretty soon, the shop opened. They had regular vacation days and sometimes the fairy would roast healthy vegetables while the siblings laid out bread and meat—although never any candy—for team dinners to build morale.

They all lived happily, for a time.

However, in the way things tend to go, their practice wasn't sustainable. The house was located too far in the woods to attract a large enough customer base. They spent a lot of money and effort trying to publicize the magical dentist office to no avail. The fairy sold the tooth house to a pair of wealthy gnomes and flew away while Hansel and Gretel headed back to town, just as destitute as before, and pretty soon their teeth once again throbbed in pain.

TRIP REVIEWS

ENDLESS FAMILY FUN!

Family-friendly good fun, with no time limit (and apparently, no actual time at all)! We boarded only moments ago but seem to have been aboard for all our lives, or at least the best we can remember! Cannot recommend this experience highly enough! (Would have given five stars if we hadn't made the mistake of thinking about Bert, which is mostly on us, we know that now).

A MEMORABLE MILLENIUM

We really had a great (actually large, grand, immense-in-scale) time spending the larger part of a thousand (1,000) solar years (0.00127 Galdraxian Chrono-Clicks) aboard (being carried by, as well as carrying within our hearts) Old Oaty. We only wish even greater (perhaps all-encompassing, -consuming, even -knowing) periods of time (as best we can agree upon a collectively-knowable definition, anyhow) were available without the mischronometric experiences reported by other (corporeal, self-contingent, non-gaseous) passengers (carried by O.O.).

IT WAS FINE

Have experienced many other choo-choo grains. This one was less coarse. Overall, the ride wasn't too rough.

(TITLE INDECIPHERABLE)

DO NOT RATE THIS EXPERIENCE!

Ugh it wont let me give it less than half a star thats so annoying, what kind of rating system is this even? How can there be a symbological system based on a numberical rating system that doesnt even go to zero or even lower maybe, what are you too cool to believe in negative numbers or what about even irrational numbers? And stars? It doesnt even specify what kind of stars were talking about here, what a sad joke. This whole rating system is just terrible and would give it negative stars if I could but since it only goes down to half a star well I guess I have to give it half a star which, insofar as this rating system is concerned, would signalize that it is just the worst.

OLD OATY IS JUST THE GORFLEB'S COMBUSTING PYJAMAS

Hot drog did we have a stellar time cruising around on Old Oaty! Not only is Oaty just the hang-doodlest thrumbumbler on the old star farm, but the views from Mt. Outlook look so far out you won't know which end is up and how to get to back.

XAVIER REYNA

WHEN I WAS A LITTLE BOY

The second son of Joseph's spinal was broken, lord knows how many
tours he had over thirteen years;
I was raised to not ask those kinds of questions
to those kinds of individuals.

And another thirteen years were spent between the shitter and the
kitchen, meaning
extra weight put excessive stress on the back.
He swings six inches above mulch every morning and every evening,
this gives him
the exercise he needs. Someone plays the clarinet, and he looks at
the men run like boys.

When I was a little boy, I was attacked by a colony of cockroaches,
I've been afraid of every genre of insect ever since.
The deer fly is the most ruthless, the lightning bug is deceptive,
the ladybug's bite is
comparable to its Cadillac cloak and the jewel wasp's sting can kill
you.

XAVIER REYNA

KOBE & HAKEEM

window ridges plant defensive architecture.
dj screw, the windows are rolled down in the summer.
speak in languages most people haven't heard of.

palm readings under palm trees.
sell cigarettes get shot, the antonyms for smoke advocates are
misleading
smoke cigarettes and write poetry.

breakfast three times a day.
love the self, live day-to-day.
kobe himself went to hakeem after winning multiple rings.

GARY GLASS

FIVE POSTCARDS FROM DINGO, WYOMING

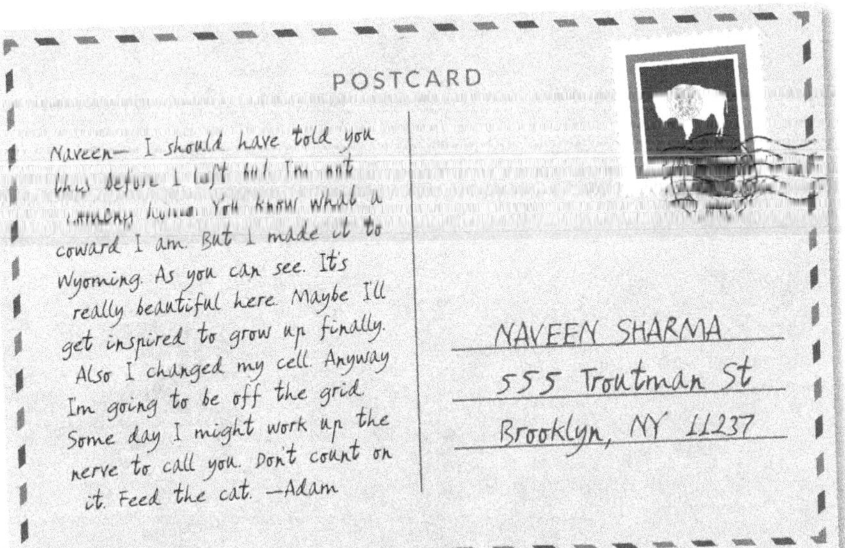

POSTCARD

Naveen— I should have told you
this before I left but I'm not
coming home. You know what a
coward I am. But I made it to
Wyoming. As you can see. It's
really beautiful here. Maybe I'll
get inspired to grow up finally.
Also I changed my cell. Anyway
I'm going to be off the grid.
Some day I might work up the
nerve to call you. Don't count on
it. Feed the cat. —Adam

NAVEEN SHARMA
555 Troutman St
Brooklyn, NY 11237

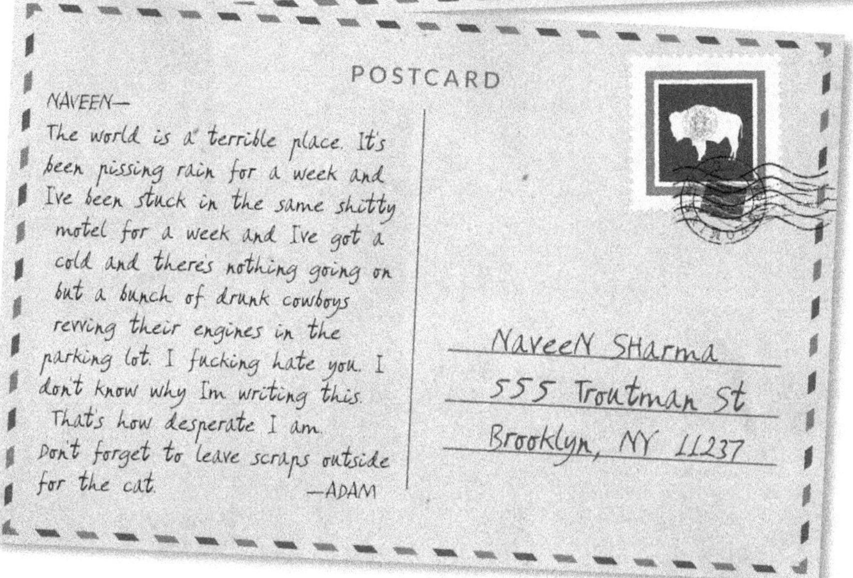

POSTCARD

NAVEEN—
The world is a terrible place. It's
been pissing rain for a week and
I've been stuck in the same shitty
motel for a week and I've got a
cold and there's nothing going on
but a bunch of drunk cowboys
revving their engines in the
parking lot. I fucking hate you. I
don't know why I'm writing this.
That's how desperate I am.
Don't forget to leave scraps outside
for the cat. —ADAM

NaveeN SHarma
555 Troutman St
Brooklyn, NY 11237

FICTION

POSTCARD

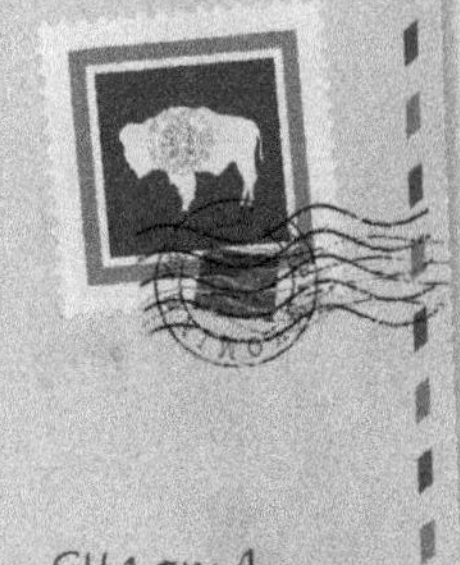

Naveen—

Wyoming is huge. It finally stopped raining so I could start my hike. That was six days ago I think. I'm lost. Also I sprained my ankle. There's no way I can ever mail this but maybe somebody will find it on my body and send it for me. I said I probably wouldn't call. Also, I apologize for calling you a fuckstick when you told me I'd die out here. You always have to be right. I hope you will take care of that poor cat. In memoriam. —Adam

Naveen SHarma
555 Troutman St
Brooklyn, NY 11237

POSTCARD

NAVEEN—

So that scene in The English Patient where Ralph Fiennes leaves Kristen Scott Thomas in the cave to die? You should be so lucky.

Some guys found me and went for help and they Medivacced me out which is when I thought about our movie. Well Im still in the hospital and Ive just noticed how much life is not like a movie. People don't go out in the wilderness and find themselves. Im still here.

Somewhere. Im sure you forgot about the cat when you thought I was dead —Adam

Naveen SHarma
555 Troutman St
Brooklyn, NY 11237

POSTCARD

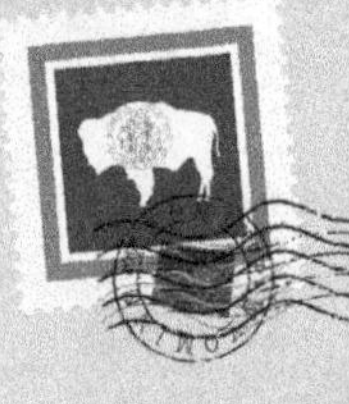

Naveen —

I was high on painkillers when I wrote you before. Whatever I said— Anyway Im staying with the couple that saved me now. They own a ranch. They're the good kind of cowboys I guess. They're teaching me to ride. I won't write to you again. Give your mother a kiss from me please. She's a crazy bitch but she was always on my side. Kiss her anyway.

Also I forgive you. cat.

—Adam

Naveen SHarma
555 Troutman St
Brooklyn, NY 11237

CONSTANCE BACCHUS

THE VULTURES RUN A WAKE, AN OLD PLASTERED GAS STATION/

i. used to be a feed store

she is a nice lady turkey vulture. refuses to rotate stocks new stuff in front. when they throw out expired goods she fills her car. there's water to drink there are so many travelers.

ii. sell hunting & fishing permits

there are payphones & party lines. a raven comes out. laughs the first time a wren runs his bike over the bell. threatens to call his parents the 3rd time. pretends to write home on an empty piece of paper.

iii. guns grandfathered in until he let them lapse/his father never let him forget it/there's always something/is monogamous

this is recent. a turkey vulture haunts the legion every night. hangs loose. walks clumsy, waddles. his spouse shows him the gun. his girlfriend drinks fast.

CONSTANCE BACCHUS

SHE HIRES A CONSPIRACY OF RAVENS

i.

there are cardboard boxes stacked w/names of cigarettes. beer flats in front by a wood framed door that can be broken & not covered by insurance. this is important.

ii.

a crow, not an environmentalist refuses to break them down. he don't pay me enough, she caws. refuses to haul them to the growing burn pile out back past the tow yard.

iii.

she is busy smoking a cigarette. blowing smoke into customers faces burning them down past the filter in the chipped ashtray on the old laminated counter above where wax paper used to roll. the eagles don't pay her any attention.

CONSTANCE BACCHUS

THE OLD CROW CLEANS THE BATHROOMS W/ BLEACH & A HOSE ONCE A WEEK/ TO KEEP THE SIGN ON THE HWY

i.

guarding her position gossips about neighbors. waiting to say no to someone looking for service who wants propane.

ii.

refuses to pump gas check oil wash windows. tells a tow victim to just pay don't fight it.

iii.

says no to people w/pennies. has forgotten they count.

CONSTANCE BACCHUS

THE CROW IS EATING CAKE NOT STOCKING

i.

she pats the dog. tosses him stick pepperoni one after the other

    a. he won't eat anything else. doesn't pay.

    b. lets him lie on the carpet in front on the counter when the vultures are looking

ii.

runs off from her husband.

    a. loses weight.

    b. her head swells.

    c. she can't fly.

iii.

comes back from a royal family back east.

    a. & when she visits still won't break the boxes down.

MICHELLE ROSS

THE CLASSIFICATION OF LIVING THINGS

THE GIRLS IN IRENE'S 1ST PERIOD biology class have formed husks. Or is the proper term rind or bark or hull? In their entombed state, the girls don't speak, so there's no getting answers from them. From within those milky, glassy threads, only the girls' eyes move. This could be looking or it could be a kind of REM.

Irene's attention is on the dry erase board when the transformation happens. Despite the boys' gasps and curses, when Irene turns, she thinks she's hallucinating. Lately, when she's in her apartment, she'll think she sees her cat Smoky out of the corner of her eye, but when she looks, nothing. Or she'll think she hears Smoky, but when she listens closely, there's only the hum of the refrigerator. Smoky has been dead two weeks. The murderer cut into the screen on Irene's porch, where Smoky spent his days watching birds flutter in the trees, his nights watching bats swoop upon mosquitos.

The boys transition quickly to curiosity. They say, "How did this happen? What does it mean?" They say, "What is the most logical conclusion?" They retrieve notebooks from backpacks and record their observations. They poke the girls' husks first with the erasered ends of pencils, then the graphite tips, then latex fingers.

They are practicing inquiry just as Irene taught them—asking questions, investigating, trying to understand.

She wants them to stop.

But she stands frozen before the dry-erase board where before class she'd written out the currently recognized domains of living things: Archaea, Bacteria, and Eukaryota. Above that she'd written out the previously recognized top of the taxa, consisting of six kingdoms; and above that the five kingdoms she'd learned as a child.

She'd wanted her students to understand how dizzyingly fast the classification of things can change as new data accrues.

Like the man in the apartment above hers after she declined his offers to change her car's oil, help unload her groceries, cook her dinner. He said to her after that last refusal, "I know you don't have a man. I know you live alone." This was at the door to her apartment. He looked not at her, but past her at the small dining table where her dinner, a maki roll, sat in its black-bottomed tray. Sometimes he didn't wait until she got into her apartment and had unloaded her things; he approached her in the parking lot as she got out of her car. For weeks, she'd made excuses for him. A bit overeager, a bit desperate, but harmless, she'd told herself. But when he said what he said about knowing she lived alone, she realized she'd been too generous. "Are you threatening me?" she said, her hand tightening on her doorknob. His eyes glinted when he said, "I'm just saying you didn't even give me a chance."

Not long after that, he called her a bitch. Then, two days before she found Smoky dead, he called her a witch. She thought witch was a slip of the tongue, that his mouth made the wrong consonant. But then he went on about all the shitty luck he'd been having—flat tire on the way to work, biting into a bitter cardamom pod, slicing his index finger on a manila folder.

A boy named Ty manages to pry a thread from a girl named Sasha's husk. Not so terrible really seeing Sasha suited up like this, Irene thinks, because always Sasha had seemed like a creature post-molt—too soft, too vulnerable. In truth, all the girls seemed too vulnerable to Irene, but some of them were better at mitigating it. Sasha, on the other hand, routinely sat hunched over her desk so that her arms shielded her breasts and her hair fell over her eyes. The effect conjured an image in one of Irene's nephew's picture books—of a cow trying to hide behind the stem of a daisy.

Irene identifies. Alone in her apartment, she feels her upstairs neighbor leering at her through his floor, the soles of his feet bearing down into her ceiling, yearning to stomp her out like a discarded cigarette butt.

If Irene were a witch, she wouldn't waste time or energy on flat tires.

Ty examines the thread under a microscope at one of the lab benches, announces that it is composed of stretched out cells like those of muscle tissue. Then he pulls at the ends of the thread, and says, "That's why it stretches," and every other boy crowds around to look.

All this poking and prodding of that thread—is it soluble? Is it conductive?—feels like misdirection. It feels too busy.

Yesterday when the restroom in the teachers' lounge was occupied by a plumber and Irene had to use the girls' restroom opposite her classroom, she thought she heard crying coming from one of the other stalls. A non-Smoky hallucination? The sound was so tiny, almost imperceptible, even though the one-minute warning bell had already rung—the hallways quieting down as students took seats in classrooms. Irene had felt afraid. Of being caught witnessing something she ought not? Of having to respond? That the situation might be more than she bargained for? That it might all be her head? Yes, yes, yes, and yes. And so she made as much noise as possible as she unrolled toilet paper, flushed, and stomped to the sink to wash her hands.

She'd felt guilty ever since. Couldn't sleep last night wondering what had happened to the girl she was now sure had been in that stall crying, the girl she pictured as Sasha with her long, acorn-colored hair shading her eyes. Irene could think of a thousand terrible things that could have happened to Sasha.

If Irene were a witch, she wouldn't waste time or energy on cardamom pods.

The boys talk of variables. They talk of cause and effect. "There's a logical explanation for this," Ty says. "We just have to figure out what it is."

Irene misses the girls' voices—how they protested when they learned that in a lion pride the females do the hunting but it's the males who eat first; how they said during the lesson on asexual versus sexual reproduction that binary fission is so much more egalitarian—every individual for her or himself.

The girls, if they could speak, would say something witty about the boys and their hacked-up-and-divvied-up thread segments, each boy's piece no more than an inch long. The girls would have something to say about the boys' focused concentration on the same damn thing, the way they look up in unison when Ty announces some new discovery, the way they quickly abandon their own investigations to repeat what their peer has already done.

The girls would have something to say about Irene's upstairs neighbor, how he thinks the universe owes him his due of various goods and fortunes—green traffic lights, tires and fingers impermeable to sharp edges, a woman. How not getting what he wants is justification for revenge.

The male police officers barely questioned her neighbor. No fingerprints. No witnesses. Nothing to corroborate her suspicion.

She shouldn't be surprised. Even when there was physical evidence and witnesses, men like her neighbor often went unpunished.

The girls are much savvier than Irene was at their age. Perhaps they're savvier than she is now. But for all their fire and wit, the girls still put up with so much they shouldn't have to. Irene worries about the excuses they, too, make and will continue to make for men and boys.

If Irene were a witch, she wouldn't waste time or energy on paper cuts.

While the boys experiment with their bits of thread, Irene sits at the empty desk next to Sasha. She looks at the girls in their translucent husks. Chrysalises, she thinks now. The girls are metamorphosizing. Why not? Caterpillars and tadpoles do it.

If Irene were a witch, she wouldn't use her magic to punish men like her neighbor. She'd make it so that they didn't stand a chance against women and girls. Let the girls emerge with thick horns, sharp teeth. Let them emerge with poison shooting eyes, hearing so keen that they can perceive a predator approaching from a mile away. Let them be fiercer than anything this world has ever seen.

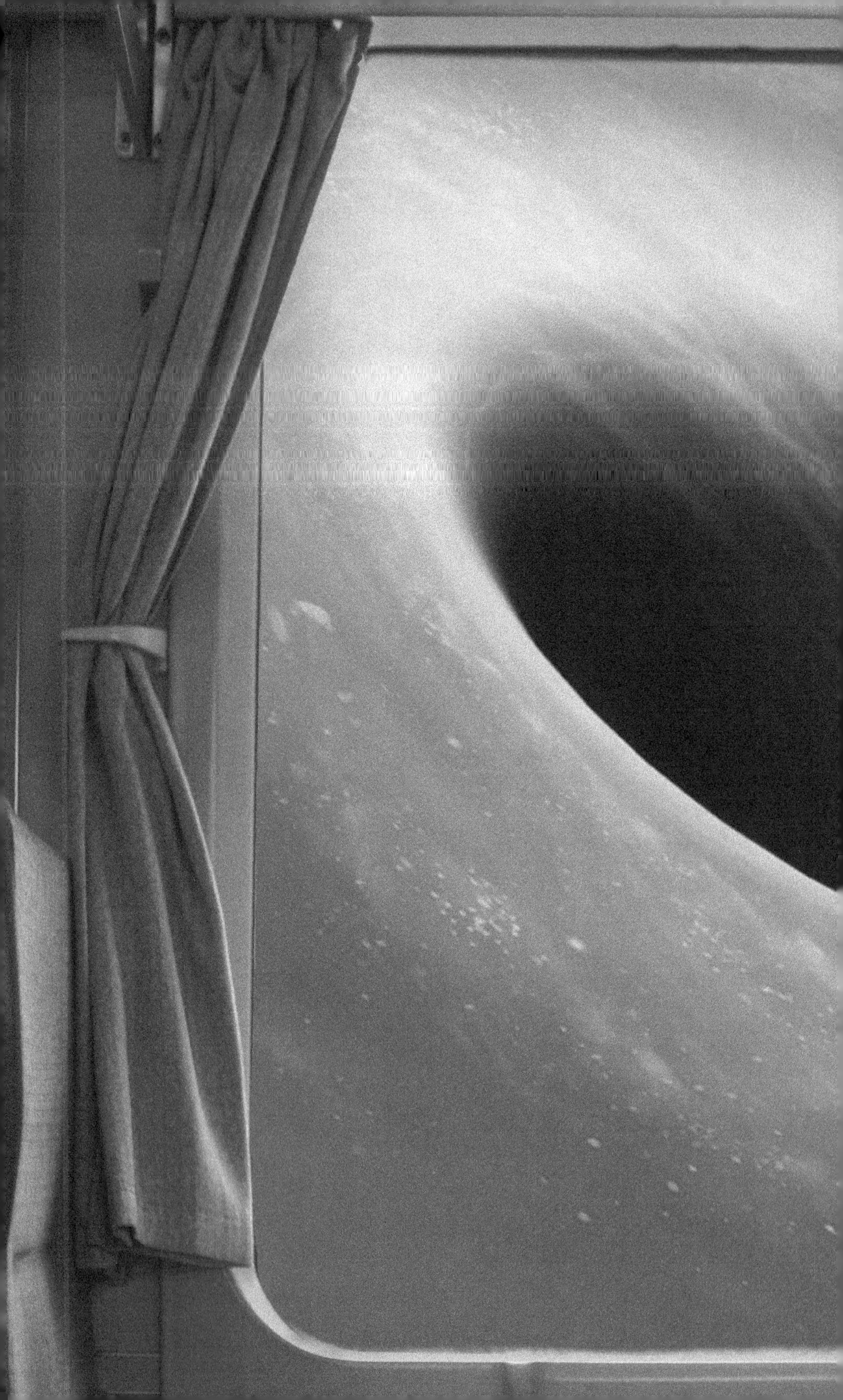

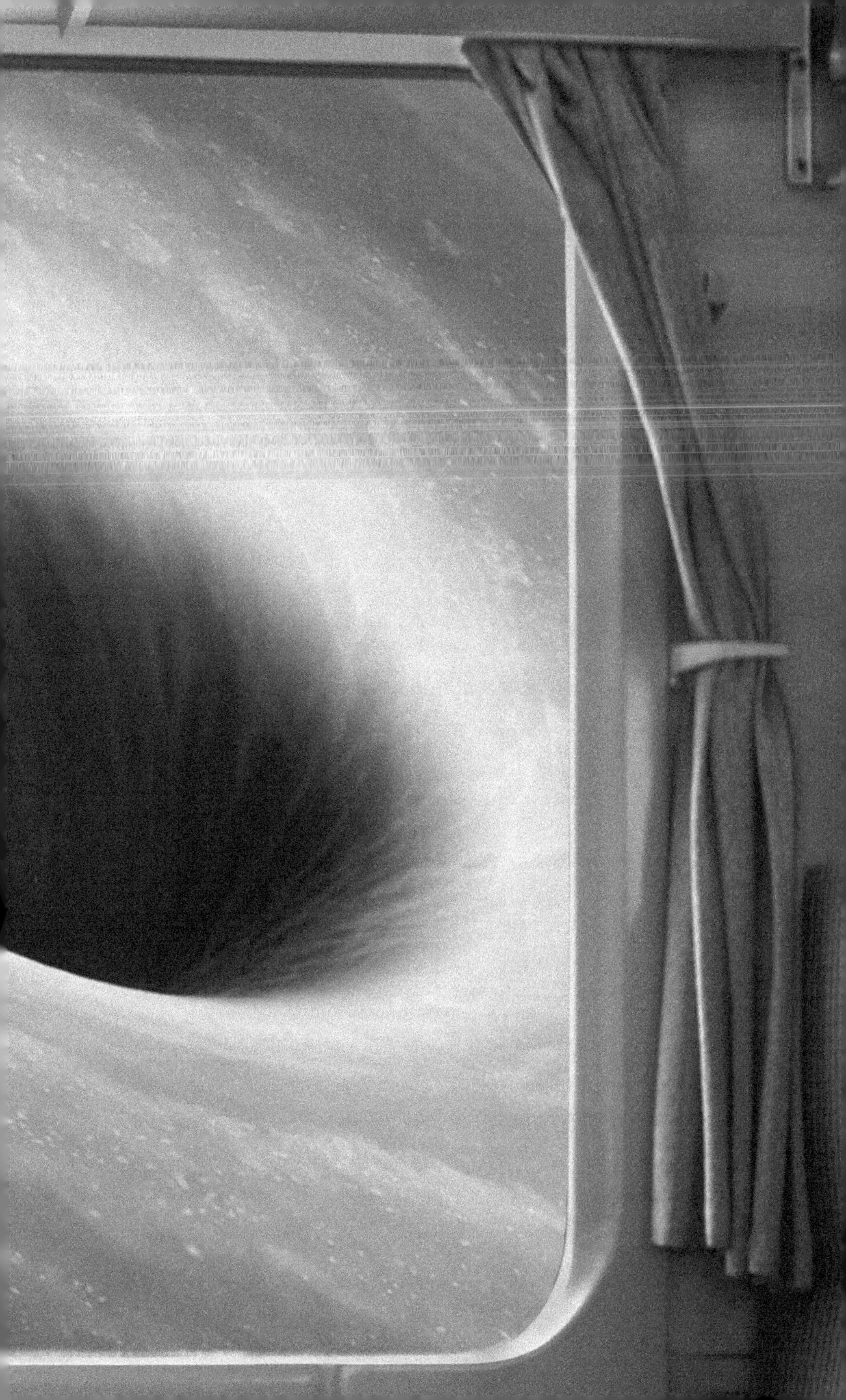

ENGINE CAM: LIVE!

● LIVE **Train Journey to Mount Outlook Summit, Autumn [1080HD] SlowTV**

1.268×10^{43} views **Octobruary 85, 2552**

Enjoy the beautiful interstellar expanses aboard the interplanetarily-renowned Old Oaty, while you get to choose your favorite timeline ...MORE

15Q Dislike Share Download Fax

157B Comments SORT BY

B **Bartleby von Stratchmore** 5,281 years ago

Wow. Just. Wow. :*)

Q **Quorg, The Infinite** Yesterday, Tomorrow, &c.

I HAVE NEVER NOT BEEN ON THIS TRAIN.
I AM LIVE STREAMING THE LIVE STREAM
WHILE ALSO BEING FOREVER ON THE ...

READ MORE

P **Pantheona P.** 12 microseconds ago

So relaxing, it's almost like my mind has liquified and oozed from my ear holes into outer space.

Infernal Hell Train AgonizinglySlowTV Endless Infinite+ Hours

Journey into the Psyche, All Aboard the Mind Train Choo Choo

JOHN RIEBOW

A PRISONER OF PORTMEIRION

2017 MARKED THE FIFTIETH ANNIVERSARY of the first airing of the seminal cult television series *The Prisoner*. Part spy drama, part psychological thriller, and part allegory, it stars Patrick McGoohan as an (unnamed) secret agent who abruptly resigns from his job with the British Secret Service. Just before the former spy can depart London, he is kidnapped and transported to a mysterious place called *The Village* where people are not known by name but by number.

But just where is The Village? Is it an island off the coast of Great Britain or in a different county altogether? Our hero, branded with the moniker Number 6 (an identity he refuses to acknowledge), spends the entire 17-episode series trying to escape his captors and outplay the mind games inflicted by a succession of administrative torturers known as Number 2. But who is Number 1? And what is so unique about The Village?

With architectural follies that are both fantasy and function, and the tidal beach where Number 6 declares, "I am not a number, I am a free man!", The Village is, in fact, the eclectic seaside resort of Portmeirion located in the northwest section of Wales, the brainchild of British architect Sir Clough Williams Ellis. Constructed between 1925 and 1975, with its odd collection of brightly painted Italianate buildings (some pieced together from the ruins of other structures), towers, and statuary, Ellis strove to create a slice of the Mediterranean in the Welsh hills. Surrounded by mountains, trees, and the sea, Portmeirion is a mini wonderland unto itself.

The actual location of The Village is not revealed until the final episode of *The Prisoner* series, and like many fans I had longed to visit the spot since first discovering the program over thirty years ago. To celebrate the golden anniversary of the drama, and make a real-world connection to the fantastical storylines, my traveling companion and I visited The Village on an adventure that took us through London, Wales, and Liverpool.

Today, The Village is managed by a trust and open to the public during the day. In the evening, the resort is closed to all but the guests of the two hotels and several dozen cottages within the property. We stayed in the Castell Deudreath, which doubled as the

Hospital in the television series, and were given room Number 6. (A coincidence?) The hotel featured an excellent gourmet restaurant, some delicious dark brown beer (Number 6 ale, of course), and a television channel that aired *The Prisoner* episodes on demand. What served as Number 6's cottage in the series now houses the obligatory gift shop, where you can stock up on all things related to the groundbreaking drama.

Besides retracing the steps of the television series, there is much to see and do in and around Portmeirion. The expansive gardens are lush and exquisite, and walking trails snake along the jagged coastline. Slightly further afield, visitors can access the Ffestiniog Narrow Gauge Steam Railway from Minffordd station, a mere mile away, where vintage steam engines transport visitors through the majestic hills and spiraling valleys of the Welsh countryside, giving stark contrast to the man-made charms of The Village. One can spend the entire day riding the trains to the slate mining town of Blaenau Ffestiniog and the coastal village of Porthmadog, sites that epitomize the term "quaint."

Portmeirion is a seven-hour train ride from London, but we broke up the journey with several overnights in local castles along the way (a story for another time). Unlike Number 6, I had a much easier time departing Portmeirion, but I would gladly become its Prisoner once again.

GET TO KNOW OLD OATY

PARTS OF THE TRAIN YOU MIGHT ENCOUNTER DURING SCHEDULED INTER-CAR PERAMBULATIONS

LOOK BUT DO NOT TOUCH

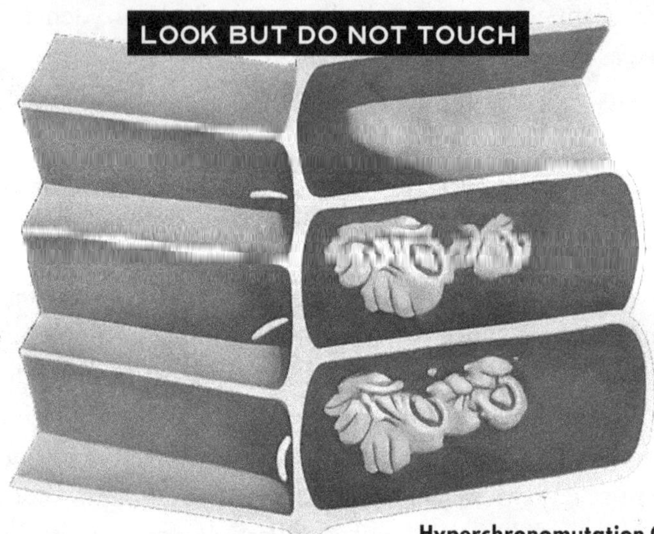

Hyperchronomutation Chambers, seen here with coalescing pre- and post-organic matter formations

SEE BUT DO NOT LOOK

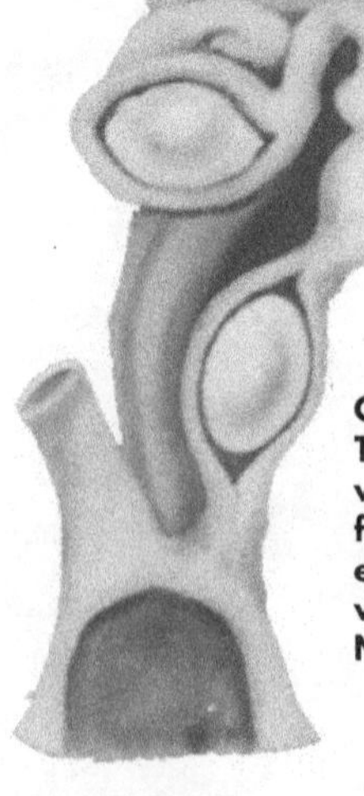

Conclobescent Thrombule, which distributes falanatory fluids extrapolemically via the Nodes of Norton

Erasmatory Refantulator, contraexpanded and primed for combustion particle expression into the anti-atmosphere

TOUCH BUT DO NOT FEEL

MICHAEL P. MORAN

2PM TELEPSYCHIATRY APPOINTMENT/F. ABELSEN/VISUAL HALLUCINATIONS TRIGGERED BY ANXIETY/POSSIBLE SYNESTHETE

No, my name is Frode Abelsen, for the 2 PM. Not Frodo, just Frode. My parents hoped life experiences would prove my name prophetic. Most parents can't fathom the cruelty of future generations or the shortsightedness of their best intentions.

You don't have to analyze that.

So, my mom told me once I should continue with my "coping mechanism" as long as it worked. You can probably figure out why I'm here now.

☎

No, the coping mechanism didn't fail; the mechanics of my mechanism did.

My mother's advice resurfaced last month when I was in the city.

"Frogger the Sponge!" John Sherman shouted in the middle of Penn Station. Sherman—thicker in the face but thinner in the hair since high school—burst with recognition. He broke his hurried stride. Wherever he was heading could wait. The prick. He hopped in sidesteps, waved gloved hands, bent low to press his grin up into my downturned face.

"Frogger! Frogger! Come on—don't you recognize me? Hey, Sponge!"

Sherman's thick fingers lunged for my world-blocking headphones and that is when I vomited a torrent of curses that staggered Sherman as if he'd been scalded. Penn Station paused. Eyes set, not on Sherman who raised his hands as if to surrender, but on me. An officer at the information desk put her D&D coffee down to fully witness the commotion. A pair of soldiers in fatigues gripped tighter the rifles in their hands.

☎

Nothing. I lowered my eyes and scurried down the stairs to platform 8, tucked myself at the back, and let the train's rocking and my headphones' songs soothe me.

☎

The nickname? It spawned naturally enough. The first day of high school, nearly twenty years ago, I had my Sony discman jammed into my sweater pocket, Freddie Mercury crammed in my ears.

☎

No, the Highlander soundtrack.

☎

Highlander? A film about immortals challenging each other to sword fights and beheading each other because there can be only one? Anyway, it's irrelevant. So, headphones on, I bolted into the road to cross six lanes of traffic with the light. Halfway across my batteries died. The crossing guard stayed with me. She took her job seriously, gloved fingers of condemnation directing cars as they rolled past the stop line beneath the traffic light. She lifted her stop sign higher, the only barrier between me and six rows of cars rumbling to move. Traffic lights cycled. The fresh pair of double-A's felt greased in my fingers. One slipped. Then the other. The green light clicked yellow, then red. Horns blared. Commuters leaned out their windows and hurled commands like javelins to drive me out of the road. I took two steps toward the curb. Retreated three steps. Spun and rushed past the crossing guard. Leapt when a car honked in aggravated bursts.

Do you see the name forming? A cluster of juniors and seniors stood across the street from the school copying homework and blowing smoke rings. So cool, right? In that particular smoke circle, Hasboro's reboot of America's favorite video game amphibian had a loyal following. One observer aimed a Newport-stained finger toward the street as cultural phenomenon crashed with the opportunity to embarrass, and the nickname emerged from the wreckage.

"Fucking Frogger!" he astutely labeled the situation.

The leap from Frode to Frogger was a joke that's lasted a lifetime.

Of course I resemble more of a toad than a frog in appearance and texture and personality. Stout arms and legs. Dry skin. Lips pulled into a grimace. Eyes severe and judgmental. None would be surprised if I were to lurch at the world and swallow it whole, drawing nourishment from the very thing I disdain.

Don't analyze that.

The moniker Frogger the Sponge followed an adolescent train of thought that I acted like a fly on the wall; urinals in the building had those fly decals to prevent "accidental spillage"; the boys aimed their piss at those stick-on flies, just like the boys aimed their jibes at me; I absorbed all the insults and Frogger taunts emptied upon me; hence, Frogger the Sponge.

On this insult, the high school boys were again severely misinformed. I didn't think myself a fly on the wall. I would've been much happier as the pink fiberglass insulation rolled between the studs and pressed on two sides by sheetrock. Forgotten. Left to disintegrate at my own pace.

Don't analyze that.

Undisturbed, that's my point.

That's not what I felt mornings on the first Tuesday of every month as I waited for the off-peak train, waited on the safe side of the yellow line that herded passengers from the ledge, waited in dark clothes with a collared shirt that—no matter how much talcum I sprinkled—chafed my neck as I assessed my peripherals. Waited

FICTION

for the train that would carry me the length of Long Island and penetrate the Big Bruised Apple like an accidental finger breaking the purpled skin.

☎

No, I don't hate the city. I hate all the people in the city. All the people on the way to the city. That's why I take off-peak one Tuesday a month.

☎

No, I'm good at my job, that's why I set the work conditions. That's not arrogance. That's truth. I made sure I landed a gig that allowed me to work from home.

☎

Home? It's quiet. That's why I like it.

☎

I never had an official diagnosis. My mom called it a sensitivity. It's more than that. More like a cursed version of synesthesia. Luckily, I was born in the right generation. College was possible because I did the whole thing online. Technology has made the life I live possible. I'm aware and grateful for that. But when they fail, these technological conveniences, I feel they fail me personally.

Don't analyze that.

☎

Again, it wasn't my headphones that failed. The inanimate world is puckish. Objects imbued with the malevolent spirits of their underpaid creators. Factory workers hardened and hateful inject spite with every staple and screw. Some will dismiss it to unfortunate circumstance when a thread catches on a chair and a new hole forms in a favorite sweater. Wrong. That's the will of some pissed laborer who—without knowing you—hates you and wants to claw at you as you pass. In this case, the metal backing on a railroad seat projected a gnarled hook and yanked. I didn't follow proper train etiquette, I admit that. I didn't allow the exiting gentleman to step off before I charged forward. Perhaps I could've avoided the calamity completely. But on the quiet car, my goal is to reach the farthest seat on the empty train. That's my seat.

☎

No. It's mine.

The old man stepped forward as I stepped forward and to avoid physical contact with him, I ducked to the side in a game of chicken neither of us was playing. That ducking brought me close enough to the gnarled hook. The headphone cord caught, tugged, then gave.

Silence is what I dread.

☎

No, dread is accurate.

I never described to my mom what it felt like. What I saw. I couldn't. She would've tried to medicate me or, worse, force me to see one of you. It begins with an itch at the elbow. No burn. A squirm, as if flies found a hole somewhere in the skin and repurposed a pocket of flesh and blood and muscle into a nursery where their hatchlings feasted and grew and writhed. As soon as the headphones went dead, I felt the squirm and considered laying my arm above the elbow on the track.

☎

No, I don't have suicidal ideations. I do have a sincere desire to sever myself from the things that bother me.

No, I couldn't just step off at the next stop. Part of me felt paralyzed at the back of the quiet car, pressed backward by invisible g-forces working solely against me. That's perception, not paranoia. When we arrived at the next stop, a woman boarded. Professional. Earbuds plugged beneath her silver bob. A battered copy of *Pride and Prejudice* protruding from her Strand Bookstore tote. A reader, a detacher. A perfect stranger to share the silence with.

Behind her slouched what I pegged as an immediate problem—an old man who cupped in his arthritic right hand a handkerchief, mostly white with a black print save for the visible wet spots where this red-nosed man deposited his sickness.

They each performed some quick geometry and determined how best to leave the most space between us. The silent reader took the center of the car; the sick man took the front. As the train lurched forward—backward for me—I felt like the kid who chose poorly the worst spot on the carnival ride and now must suffer the weight and force of his corndog-fattened friends.

I'm not paying to talk about friends.

The headphones, without sound, accomplished nothing. The pneumatic train brakes bored through the headset padding. Instinctually I plugged two pointer fingers into my ears, just the fingers' pads. I crossed my middle fingers over them and pressed in to seal the holes. Five minutes in my fingers started cramping. I considered hiding out in the bathroom, but the out-of-order sign discouraged me.

No, I'm not easily discouraged. I just didn't want to try if I thought I had no chance of succeeding. Don't analyze that.

Not thirty seconds since our departure, old Mr. Sickness rumbled a few phlegmy tremors. Again and again. Haeyum. Haeyum. The sound of a forced breath tickling mucus and gargling hot spit. Look, this is where I invoke confidentiality. You can't tell anyone about this, okay?

It was like each eeuhhm, eeuuhhm, eeeuhhhm was a call for attention, a way for this skeletal nothing of a person to occupy more space in the car, another malignant creation. Look at me, look at me, it demanded. I've survived countless recessions, a few remissions, I've buried or burned everyone I've known and loved, and now I'm the nearly extinct last of my bloodline.

Eeuuhmm. Eeeuuuhhm. Euuuuhhhm.

With each tremor, the old man placed his handkerchief to his mouth to catch the wetness gathered at his lips. I've seen old men pulling stringy spit threads from their lips before. Gross, sure, but not something so bad I would charge my debit card for your services. That saliva silk isn't what caught my attention. Before he dabbed his lips, he dropped his jaw as his throat opened, and that's when I saw something in his mouth reflecting the light pouring into the train. A passing glimmer covered by the handkerchief.

Another cough and this time I saw an eye darting side to side in his maw before it turned its gaze on me.

☎

No. You think I'd be talking to you if it were a gumball or a piece of hard candy he chiseled off a mound he keeps in a saucer at home? This was a human eye, still in the socket!

☎

Just because it's impossible doesn't mean it was impossible for me to see.

That's how all this works. Or doesn't work.

Finally, the old guy broke up something in his chest, churned up substance from the back of his throat, turned his head to the right and spat into his handkerchief. I'm sure some particle landed in that filthy white rag, but next to him landed something bigger and nastier. It was covered in slime green and yellow, but I could still make out the red nose.

☎

There were two. Two old men now. The sick guy who kept clearing his throat and another version of the sick guy he spewed out his mouth. It landed with a slap in the open chair like puking a human slug half the size of the original, but identical in likeness and manner. The guy brought his handkerchief to his red honker and the slimy dwarf version of him brought his up too. They turned opposite each other and sneezed in unison.

Ever see Gallagher? The comedian. Sledgehammer guy? He'd place various pieces of fruit on a table and smash them with a sledgehammer. Chunks of watermelon would fly five rows deep. Picture that, but with a bag of overripe avocados.

Neither one of the guys caught their explosive globs so in each droplet that pooled on a seat or oozed down the window, a little tadpole version of the old man swam. And now all of them—ALL. OF. THEM.—were hacking at a new cough, each gagging on a smaller version to regurgitate onto an empty seat.

The train car was completely compromised and spreading.

☎

No, I wasn't afraid of getting sick. I'm not a hypochondriac. Each human emission merely filled the car a little more.

No, the woman didn't see it. I wouldn't have seen it either if my headset worked.

No, I don't like those cordless headsets. Don't trust them. Forget to charge them one night, and where does that leave me? And forget those ridiculous noise canceling monstrosities. There's no discretion. Everyone knows I'm trying to silence them.

No, I just don't want the attention.

At the next stop a guy got on and nearly slipped on all that mucus. He may have just lost his balance. He was older. You'd guess not a speck of tech on him, but poking out of his shirt pocket was a small screen, some early model iPhone he probably used to look at pictures of his grandkids and play Bubblewrap. He was another reader, but the worst kind. Not one, not two, but three—THREE!—physical newspapers tucked under his arm. This was the man keeping the print industry alive and I wanted to kill him.

He kept a tight grip on the paper despite his arthritis-swollen knuckles. As if he had lost so much already and feared one rogue breeze could steal his morning routine, his final connection to the world of the living.

He folded the *Times* proper, just enough to read the top story above the fold, but each time he shifted a cheek to ease the pressure on his flagrant hemorrhoids, the paper crinkled in his grip.

That's when I saw them, falling like termites from the printed page. They marched across his lap, a miniature army of retirees wandering, lost, bumping into and pardoning each other. He was crawling with these pests. They spilled out of his lap, scuttled along and down the leg of his chair, moved with the chaos of a nest disturbed by some misplaced foot.

He looked about, unaware of his personal infestation, noted the freedom of riding the quiet train off-peak and decided to set himself up as if he were seated at his kitchen table. He rested his deli coffee next to him, leaned back against the chair, and with the gesture of a magician revealing the full breadth of his cape, snapped his wrists to unfurl the Times' full area. The little maggot creatures flung from the pages. Some struck the windows and splattered, then dripped down. Others landed in clumps on surrounding seats and wriggled over each other.

Again and again, SNAP SNAP SNAP, like wind against the sail of a ship destined for destruction, sucked down into a watery pit, the crew marked as crab grub and future sand particles.

How does he not hear it? The crinkle and shimmy of his eyes bobbing down the page like a Plinko disc.

☎

Plinko. Remember? I'm not sure if they still have that game on the show. The contestant stood atop this huge plastic and pressboard game and dropped a disc down, hitting wood nubs that sent the disc in different directions. They could aim as much as they wanted over the prized center slot, but one bounce could "rob" them of thousands of dollars and drop them in a cold zero-dollar outcome. It didn't rob them; the prize was never theirs to begin with. Only humans lose things they never had. I quit watching that pre-afternoon guilty pleasure when Bob Barker retired.

☎

I don't know, do I have difficulty adjusting to change?

On the train it was a slow change. The walls and floor were pulsing with convulsive creatures, asexual beings pregnant with sound.

☎

No, I don't want to talk about my sex life. That would be more of an epitaph than a conversation. Have you ever tallied all the sounds made during sex? If people could see sounds the way I do, they'd yank out their tongues and slipper their feet and never again disturb the air with their noise. Do I remind you of the Grinch, up there on Mount Crumpit hating the Whos with all their noise, noise, noise, noise? A more realistic scenario, less Suessian, would involve the Grinch loading up his sled with explosives and aiming it down the mountain at that Who circle surrounding the tree so the last things he heard were their screams and calls to whatever deities Whos worshipped until all was snuffed out with flame and silence.

☎

No, I don't seriously entertain these thoughts. I've also never considered blinding myself to avoid seeing the world this way. I do, however, blast songs in my headphones, hoping the caution on the phone comes true—listening to music at high volumes may cause permanent hearing damage. But other than that, I've never considered plunging a Q-tip down my ear canal either.

Patior ergo sum, right? Don't analyze that.

I was halfway to the city and I hoped—maybe—with these visions filling the car at their geriatric pace, I could arrive, hold tight, and return home unscathed. Fire off an email on the ride back and reschedule the meeting for the next day. Diarrhea, I'd tell them. No one questions that. But then I heard a flutter of demon wings. The lady with the silver bob laid her book open in her lap and lifted from her tote the buzzing source to terrorize me. Her eyes flashed with

FICTION

recognition and a devilish grin curled her lips.

"Hellllll O?" she whispered but didn't. "I was hoping we could have a con-ver-sa-tion." She broke the last word into bits like a witch dismembering a gingerbread man.

She released a laugh that required nothing of her lips or teeth or tongue, a high-pitched hum smothered at the back of her throat. From her mouth popped a spit bubble, and from that bubble erupted a winged thing. It perched above her on the luggage rack. Its hair silver, eyes black with impish impulse. It snaked leathery arms through the metal bars of the rack, hooked long fingers behind her front teeth, slapped a reptilian hand on her chin, then winked at me. It pried her head nearly in half and cracked its own face to match. Together they cackled, a discordant whirr that summoned a swarm. Google "Asian giant hornet" and let your nightmares commence. Thousands of them, wrinkled pixies colliding and swirling into a funnel directed toward me.

What could I do? I closed every orifice my muscles could constrict. Every voluntary sphincter pinched. I pressurized my nose to restrict access to my lungs. She corrupted the air with malignant laughter. Each punchline launched the hornet-demons like darts. Even with my eyes closed I felt them penetrating my skin. She attempted to bite her laughs to decrease her disruption, and those clicking teeth became the clack of her spawns' abdomens pumping deeper and deeper their venom.

I curled my legs and buried my face in my knees. I bit my lower lip and rolled my ear lobes to plug my ear canals. Rode all the way to Penn that way, like a human pill bug.

You've seen them. Some folks call them roly-polies. Their main defense is to curl into a ball when threatened. Of course that defense does absolutely nothing to spare them from becoming a gray smear under my Converse.

No, I don't find pleasure in killing bugs, though technically pill bugs are crustaceans. Feast on that next time you slurp up shrimp Alfredo at the Olivo Garden. The point is this. I feel a connection to those little doodlebugs tucked into themselves to avoid the world.

I rode home that way too. Flashed my monthly pass at the assistant conductor, didn't even pull my head from between my knees. Ordered four sets of headphones on Amazon as soon as I got home. But that's not enough.

Every sound births a sound births a sound. The offspring of careless coughs and free-wielded laughter overpopulate the space around me until it feels a bit like drowning (I'd imagine). That physical weight, that pressure. To breathe is to die. To suffocate is to die too. What would you prefer? To be deprived of air or overcome with fluids?

The weight of sound? I don't know, but when I was a kid my favorite part of swimming was sinking and letting that chlorinated water fill and pressurize my ears. I don't float. No buoyancy. I'd pull a dead man's float for about ten seconds before my legs would swing down. I'd bob then sink. Everything that troubled me would vanish—the lifeguard's sharp whistles, the dumb throb of children testing the diving board's limits, the slaps of sunscreen from mothers anxious to protect their uncooperative brats. Do you have any meds like that? I want to sink into silence without dying.

☎

You mean life or death? No, but that doesn't mean it's not an emergency. You can just send a script to the CVS near my house. I'll give you the address. They deliver.

☎

Is that a law or your own personal preference?

☎

Where's your office?

☎

Are you fucking kidding me?

BERNADETTE GEYER

PARABLE OF THE MIRACLE TREE

And lo,
there appeared in the tree in the nursing home lobby
a set of dentures, which fit the mouth of one resident
as if it were his own. He bit. And the biting was good.

The next day,
there appeared in the tree a pair of spectacles, lenses round
as the world and ground to focus the sight of one who but
for them would be blind. And her sight begat belief.

Photos of loved ones began to alight on the branches
along with charms and trinkets, the occasional shoe.
Nothing was ever lost that the tree did not give back to them.

It came to pass
they called it Miracle Tree and worshipped, numb
with wonder, beneath the laden branches.

Hearing aids. Amlodipine. Capsaicin tablets. A lock
of hair clutched by a nearly translucent silk ribbon.
Daily, the tree filled with what was necessary.
Daily, the residents rejoiced at their blessings.

FORMS OF WHICH TO BE COGNIZANT

COSMIC TRANSIT REVEALS ALL KINDS OF FUN FORMS TO THE UNGUARDED MIND!

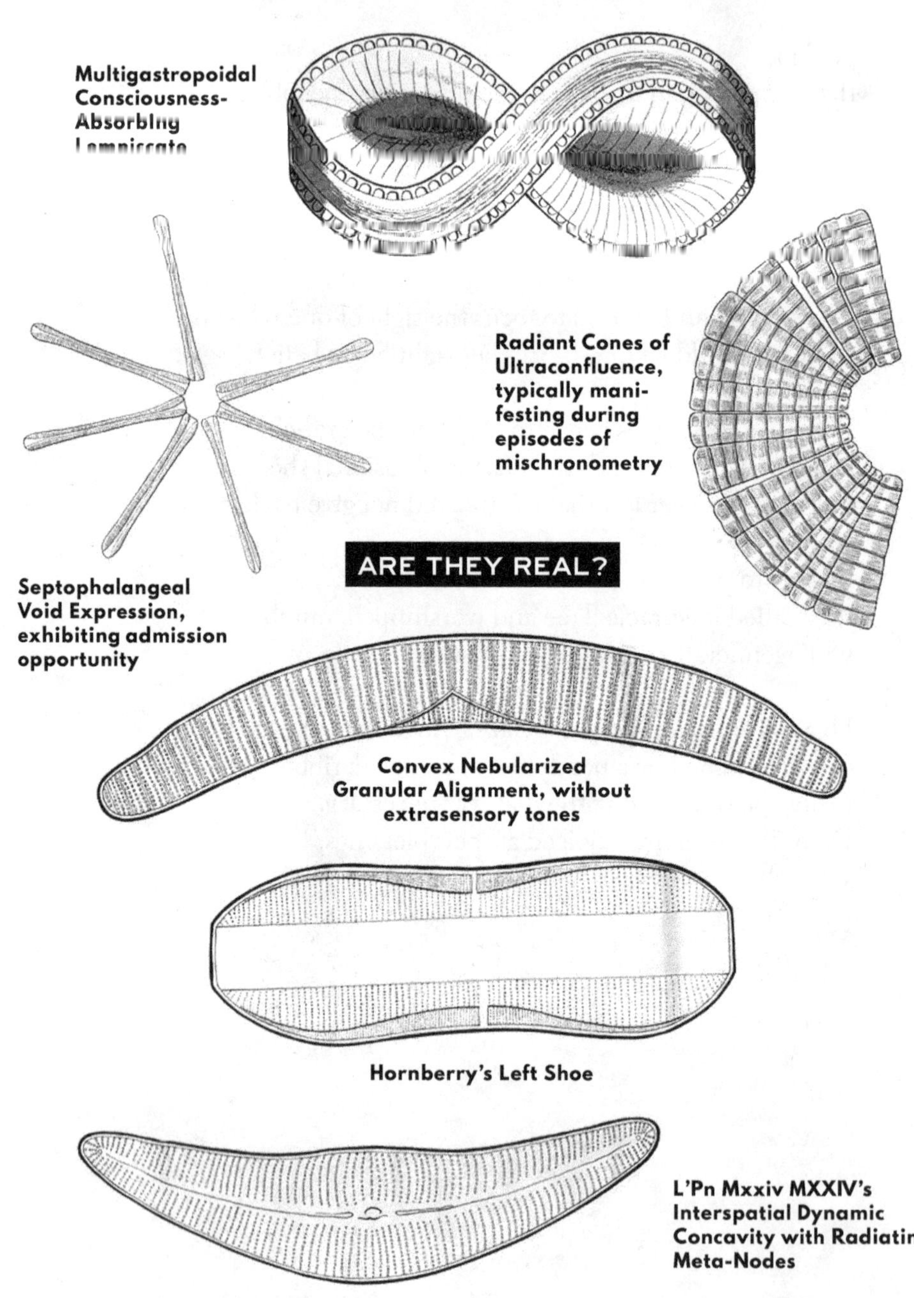

MARISA CRANE

SIREN ISLAND

Once again it was DoubleDeath™ Saturday which meant you could die twice for the price of one. I was captaining the ship on the second go-around and the crewmates—a group of 50 something men who'd never fully let go of their frat boy days—were dripping red dye all over my new sea boots, which I'd had to beg Mr. Peterson to buy even though everyone could see my socks through the holes in my old ones. Not much respect for me around these parts, but whatever, I had new boots. I asked Crewmate #1 or Crewmate #5 or whoever was standing closest to me if he could climb to the crow's nest to "get a better view of the island." He complied with a huff that said he was a paying customer who shouldn't be bossed around, even if it was literally my job to boss him around. A job—I must admit—that was a source of pride! I'd been working at Siren Island for four years before I got promoted to Captain. Imagine, me, a captain!

I fixed my hat with one hand while I spun the helm left, then right, then another right. I didn't have to steer—the boat was attached to a track—but I liked to play my role to the best of my ability. Why do something if you weren't going to give it your all? The first note over the loud speaker signaled it was time to recite my lines.

"Do I hear singing? The most beautiful singing I've ever heard in all my terrible life?" I said, raising my voice so all the men could hear.

I signaled Lonely Lou to turn the wave machine up and soon waves were slapping against the side of the ship like an angry ex with liquid courage.

"Oh, fuck yeah," said Crewmate #2, red dye dripping down the front of his shirt. He blocked the sun with his hand and peered at the rocks where the sirens sunbathed, their skin slick with sweat and chlorinated water.

"These bitches are hot and ready for us," said Crewmate #5.

I didn't like how these men were speaking about the sirens and not sure how to best handle the situation. These weren't the usual clientele of submissive men in pleated slacks and ill-fitting glasses, men who secretly wished a woman would step on their necks but were so afraid of real pain they settled for a simulation. I didn't think they'd respond to reprimands, so I tried redirecting them, once again pointing out the sirens' beautiful, ethereal singing voices.

"We must go to them at once!" I announced, the boat pulling a quick left directly toward the island.

"Hey, whores!" Crewmate #1 called to the sirens. They busied themselves pretending to play their string instruments.

"Please refrain from using offensive or derogatory language!" I said, my voice chipper but fraught with fury.

"We're only playing. It's make-believe," said Crewmate #2, approaching me. His defensiveness wafted off him like a fart.

I don't know why they felt comfortable speaking about women that way in front of me. Maybe they thought I was a man. At the time I had a short 90s heartthrob cut and they kept pestering me to join the taunting. Instead, I yelled, "Ahoy, mates, I see enemies to the West!"

It was no use. Crewmate #2 turned to the West but merely shot a snot rocket onto the deck I'd literally just cleaned after the first go-around.

The sirens were really something, I'm not going to lie. Mr. Peterson had a knack for hiring. Sure, their outfits were only a step above a child's homemade Halloween costume—a slip-on set of bird wings and beaks—but the women wearing them were real knockouts. Fat women, thin women, muscular women, all with this fierce look like they couldn't wait to crush your skull. Out of all the sirens, though, Sara was the star. We'd hardly spoken during our years working together but rumor was she'd been an Olympic swimmer back in France. She had these big eyes and big lips and cheekbones you could cut your hand on. People hung pin-ups of her in their homes. She was our cash cow. It wasn't a secret that she was keeping us afloat.

Spotting the boat, the sirens climbed down from their rocks onto the sand and waded into the sea, doing this seductive dance, limbs loose and wild. The men grabbed their crotches, gyrating so fast I thought their hips might break. Somewhere the ghosts of murdered sailors were watching this mockery.

Was nothing—not even being lured to death by mythical creatures—sacred?

The waves got rough at this point, so I said my next line: "Oh, no, a storms a'brewin', don't know if this baby will make it!"

My siren friend Gabriela got down on all fours and slithered toward the ship, hissing and spitting like something rabid. She winked at me. Our own private conversation. We'd been friends for quite a while. It was nice having someone to commiserate with.

The men ignored me and began to hoot and holler. Even though I wasn't a real captain I still felt a sting in my heart. I wanted to be appreciated. Who didn't?

Because of their carrying on, I got distracted and forgot to pull the brake that ensured we'd "crash" slowly and safely onto the island. We hit the beach hard, the jolt sending everyone flying forward onto their faces and hands. Me, I fell awkwardly into the helm, and was nursing quite a bruised sternum. Only then did I pull the emergency brake and turned the ship off.

"What the fuck, man?" Crewmate #2 said. "That didn't happen the first time," he said. At first, I thought he was upset, but he was giddy with adrenaline.

All the other guys agreed that was "fucking awesome" and that I was the best captain around. Me, the best captain around! I couldn't wait to tell Mr. Peterson. He'd surely give me that raise I'd been gently nudging him about.

The sirens behaved as if nothing were out of the ordinary and descended upon the ship like always. I'd never known people's bodies to move like that. They clawed at the side of the ship, lip-syncing to music playing over the loudspeakers. When I'd first been hired, as a janitor, Mr. Peterson had been determined to hire hot sirens who could also sing but he soon learned that hot women with even a lick of singing talent usually ended up famous, not working at Siren Island. We settled for Icelandic recordings from YouTube. We figured the foreign language would make the music sound more mysterious.

One by one, the men jumped into the water and threw themselves at the sirens. It was clear they each had a favorite. I was scripted to warn that these creatures were dangerous, that they couldn't be trusted, but I didn't. I was trying not to panic. The ship's ON switch wouldn't work. We were stuck. I'd broken the ship.

Through tears I watched the sirens transform from seductresses into evil beasts. Red dye spilled everywhere as they "ripped" the men's hearts out of their chests. The men were practically cumming in their pants which is great for customer reviews, but I was too busy imagining the cruel things Mr. Peterson would say when he discovered I'd broken his ship. I didn't even notice that Sara had somehow evaded the men, climbed onto the ship, and was speaking to me.

"Marry me," she said with the annoyance of someone who'd already repeated themselves.

Even then, I didn't respond. I like to think I was coming up with a clever response, but I think I was in shock.

"I need a green card," she said.

"What do I get?" I asked.

"Well," she said, gesturing to her body. "This."

That, I had trouble arguing with.

The next morning, Mr. Peterson called me to his office. He'd heard about my shipwreck blunder, about Sara's proposal.

"You're going to marry her, right?" he said.

"I mean, I don't know?" I told him how my mom had always taught me to marry for love, that even a queer kid like me could achieve that. I sounded so pathetic but as I spoke of love, I thought of Gabriela which unsettled me. I needed to focus on my job and my well-being!

Mr. Peterson said, "What a beautiful story—" I started to say that my mom was one of the good ones but he bulldozed right over me. "—that I don't give a rat's ass about."

"Understood," I lied, thinking of Gabriela. She was stunning, of course, and she was also a bookworm, which I loved. She was kind and funny, too—generous even. One time she'd rescued my credit card after I'd forgotten it at Pacific Shores, drunk from too many shots celebrating Siren Island's five-year anniversary. She was all I could think about since Sara proposed. But then I saw it. I was in love with her. Facing a marriage proposal is an inopportune time to realize you're in love with someone else.

FICTION

Mr. Peterson lit a cigarette. "If you don't marry Sara, she's going to get deported." He took a drag and blew the smoke at the ceiling. "We will certainly go under without her. We'd lose all her regulars. You don't want that, do you? Don't you love your job here at Siren Island? Hell, I just promoted you to captain. Don't you want to keep that job?"

I told him that yes indeed, I did want to keep this job.

"Which is why you're going to marry her," he said. "Right, Alicia?"

"Right, boss."

"Say it with me now," he said.

I stared at him.

"I," he said.

I kept staring. Where was Gabriela now? Probably ripping some poor bastard's heart out.

"I," he repeated several more times until I finally joined in.

"I. Will. Marry. Sara," we said slowly, as if trying each word on for size.

"That's what I thought," he said. "Glad we cleared that up."

I thought that was it but when I turned toward the door, he told me to wait. I turned around, hoping for I don't know what.

"And happy engagement," he said, raising his eyebrows.

I left his office feeling lower than I had in a long time.

Outside Mr. Peterson's office, Sara was smoking a cigarette by the bathrooms. She looked effortlessly cool. I gave her a small wave and headed to the locker room to change into my captain costume. She followed me, although I didn't realize it until I closed my locker to find her standing in front of me, ass naked.

"Told you this is what you get," she said.

I tried not to look at the parts I very much wanted to look at. She seemed very confident but perhaps that was a front for her anxiety? Whether I would accept her proposal or not. Whether she'd have to go back to France. She must not have talked to Mr. Peterson yet.

Sara cupped her breasts in her strong, vascular hands. It struck me that she was performing for me in the same way she did our paying customers. A cool, slinky version of herself. I thanked her—not for anything specific—just the words *thank you.* She gave me this weird look.

"You remind me of a record played backward," she said. "Like a secret message."

Then she went down on one knee and proposed again. She told me she loved me and that she'd never met anyone like me. Not in the whole god-forsaken world.

I'm not stupid, I knew she didn't love me, but I found myself softening with every word nonetheless. Stupid, stupid idiot.

I must have been smiling because she said, "So, you'll do it then, yes?"

Sara had this way of finishing every sentence with a question that only had one correct answer. I asked her how long we'd have to stay married.

"A few years, at least. But we could stay together forever. Free to do whatever we want but always have someone nice to come home to," she said. "You're nice, aren't you?"

"I'm probably not the best judge of that."

"Well, you are," she said. "You are."

I asked her if this sort of thing was illegal.

"Only if we get caught," she said.

"Only if we get caught," I repeated.

As a pathological rule-follower, I couldn't even bring myself to wear socks in the locker room on account of Mr. Peterson's SHOES ONLY sign. The mere thought of breaking an actual law had me sweating straight through my shirt.

Sara and I left the locker room together and ran straight into Lonely Lou. All 6 ft. 7 in. of him. He said he heard the good news from Boss and already put a call in to Pacific Shores to let them know we'd be having a huge engagement party the following night.

"Come on in, folks. Let's celebrate two lovely ladies in style. Love is love! And all that good stuff!" Lou waved his arms like an air traffic controller ushering everyone into an imaginary bar.

Even as it was all happening, it felt like this had always been my life and I had never known anything else.

After work, the night before my engagement party (*my engagement party!*), I called up my mom to tell her the news. We're very close and I didn't want her to hear it from anyone else. My cousin Rachelle worked in the marketing department and it would be so-Rachelle to tell my mom first. I'd never lied to my mom. She knew me in and out and knew I wouldn't be into a showboat who sucked up all the oxygen in the room. A stud who knew she was a stud. Someone I'd previously described to my mother as *callous* and *unapproachable*. So I waited for her to answer her phone so I could tell her I was going to marry

FICTION

a callous, unapproachable, showboating stud who sucked up all the oxygen in the room. That said, my mother had never married and me marrying had always been one of her goals.

She answered on what seemed like the last ring. I guess it's always the last ring.

I told her I had something to tell her, could she please balance on one leg (That was our thing; instead of sitting down for news, we pretended to be flamingos.)

"What is it, Leesh?" This poor woman.

I told her about Sara and the sudden engagement party. I waited for her to accuse me of something. Of lying, of withholding my dating life, of proposing to someone without telling her first. Something. Instead, she squealed the squeal of twenty-seven moms exploding into a chorus of, "I CAN'T BELIEVE THIS IS HAPPENING! OH MY GOD, MY BABY IS GETTING MARRIED!"

I'd yanked the phone away from my ear so I almost missed that she said she would leave as soon as possible. "I'll drive through the night. It's only nine hours from Monterey!"

"That's not necessary, Mom. The party isn't until tomorrow night."

"You don't have the faintest idea how parenthood works," she yelled.

"You're right about that," I said.

We hung up and Sara texted me to come check out her apartment since I'd obviously be moving in there. She used words like *spacious* and *modern* and *refined* and *curated*. I only cared about the word *spacious* since I liked having room to dance. I wasn't a particularly good dancer but something about moving my body soothed me. No one could tell you how to move, not even the music. This was especially true if you were white, which I am.

Only after I agreed to visit Sara's did I realize that my apartment was also spacious and in a central location, walking distance to bars and restaurants and shops, and only a short drive to work. Why hadn't I mentioned that? Out the door I went, a bottle of wine in tow. I kept

FICTION

finding myself pulled in a particular direction. This is what it must have felt like for sailors who were unwittingly lured to their deaths. Great, I was now method acting.

I first met Sara five years ago at Pride. I was freshly out of a relationship with a woman who'd been very good to me, who I regretted leaving every day. Sara was topless with heart-shaped rainbow pasties over her nipples, dozens of fans surrounding her with Sharpies requesting her to sign various parts of their bodies. Those without a Sharpie were pawing at her, desperate for a little skin-to-skin. She emerged from the sea of worshippers and was suddenly in front of me introducing herself. Maybe she wanted me to laugh and say that I, of course, already knew who she was, but the truth was—I didn't—so I waited for her pitch.

"Come with me." She grabbed my hand. "I want to show you something." Everyone watched as she pulled me through the crowd. Someone reached out, touched my face, and yelled "I touched the face of the person touching Sara!"

Sara sat me in front of a tarot card reader. "Your life is out there waiting for you. If only you will acknowledge it." She handed the tarot card reader some cash then sauntered to the bar where she took a shot that had been lit on fire. All those hands on her, yet she was untouchable. When my reading was done—the woman told me it was going to be a big year, that I should say yes to opportunity—Sara waved me over. She told me I looked like I needed a change. Then she offered me a shot and a job at Siren Island.

As far as I could tell, Sara's apartment was all those words she'd used but I couldn't get over the fact that I was going to be moving in with this person who was to become my wife. I handed Sara the bottle of

FICTION

red to open and she poured two generous glasses. On the wall hung a 36x48 photo of her in a swim cap and bathing suit in position on a starting block. The angle of the shot made it look like Sara was about to dive straight into you.

"Are you excited about our party?" She said it like we were really lovers taking the leap.

I didn't answer.

"Did you tell your family?" she said. "Do you have family? I suppose that's something I'll need to know for the interview."

I told her that I'd called my mother, that she was on cloud nine about the whole thing. I told Sara she better be good at acting because I wanted my mom to believe this, that I was deserving of love. Sara furrowed her brow then took a long drink.

"It's not that big of a deal," she said. "People do this all the time."

"Okay," I said.

"If you want to blame anyone, blame your country."

"Okay. But—okay. But I am in love with Gabriela and now I've lost my chance to tell her!"

Sara blinked slowly, raised her hand to the stem of my glass and tipped it back, pouring the wine down my throat. When both glasses were gone, she refilled them and drank thoughtfully for a moment. "What does marriage have to do with love?"

I didn't have an answer for that so instead I asked, "Why me? Out of all the people you could have chosen?"

"What do you mean? You're one of my best friends," she said.

This was news to me. We hadn't had more than ten conversations in the four years since Pride. Sara must be lonelier than Lonely Lou lost at sea.

Pacific Shores was packed when my mom and I rolled up. Sara said she'd meet us there, which hadn't instilled confidence that she could

pull off pretending to love me for my mother's sake. I imagined the immigration officer breathing down my throat.

"What you're telling me is your own fiancée *met you* at your engagement party?" they'd say.

"My hands are tied," they'd say.

"Do you see what kind of message you're sending?" they'd say.

This conversation would inevitably end with me getting fined $10,000 and thrown in prison until my hair turned gray.

My mom must have been in cahoots with the imaginary officer because she asked what type of person meets their fiancée at their own engagement party. I told her a siren; a siren is just the type.

"What? Are you drunk already?"

"Sirens can't be bargained with," I said.

"Sirens aren't real, honey."

"Okay, Mom," I said. "Okay, okay, okay."

We squeezed through a crowd of older gay men clutching cocktails who'd been there since it was The Porch, a gay dive bar. Pacific Shores wasn't much of a gay bar anymore, but the gays went there anyway, unwilling to let go. We took off our jackets and threw them over a high top. I was wearing my favorite button-down and a bow tie. They would later be ruined.

"Gosh, I'm just so happy you're happy!" My mom's cheeks flushed with emotion. Her earnestness was enough to make me cry. Any part of me that hadn't already been broken shattered in that moment.

It was still early but people were already pretty toasty. A few were aiming popcorn into each other's mouths, swaying on their stools as they dove. One man rubbed popcorn into his armpits. Pacific Shores didn't sell real food, but you could eat as much popcorn as you wanted, but you'd only get one or two cups before the machine was empty. No one bothered to refill it. Pacific Shores must have liked people falling on their asses and having threesomes in the bathroom. It seemed to be a part of their branding.

Lonely Lou was standing on a small stage, microphone in hand. That's what happens when you're an old Porch regular; they let you bring your own laptop and speakers for karaoke. Say what you want about Lonely Lou, but he loved him some karaoke. It was about the only thing he'd talk about and he'd talk your ear off.

Sitting at a table with another siren was Gabriela. She gave me a little wave, but her mouth was a straight line, eyes big and questioning. My mom followed my gaze then raised her eyebrows at me.

"Just a friend from work," I said defensively.

"She looks like someone who just missed the last train home."

"What the hell is that supposed to mean?" It wasn't like me to be this snappy with my mom. I was floating further and further away from myself with each breath.

Thankfully she ignored me, scouting the room with her hand over her eyes like a visor. "I could be a sailor, too, you know. An important part of navigation is to block out all distract—oh, oh, I think I see your lover!" She shoved my shoulder like an excited schoolgirl.

We crossed the bar, peeling through drunk bodies until we were standing in front of Sara, chatting with Mr. Peterson. Some eager fans pointed and whispered nearby. I wasn't sure what to do, how to greet her, but I figured touching would have to be involved. I didn't realize how drunk she was until she turned to me. Her eyes were all squinty like she was trying to read the fine print on my face.

"Alicia," she said, as if she'd just recently learned my name.

"Sara," I said. "This is—"

Before I could finish introducing my mom, Sara grabbed my face with both hands and laid a big, sloppy kiss on my lips, saliva smearing all over my mouth in indiscriminate patterns like a kid's splatter painting. When she finally pulled away, my mom was grinning with several years' worth of serotonin flooding her synapses.

"We were just talking about you, weren't we?" Sara said, glancing at Mr. Peterson.

"That we were," he said, giving me a paternal smile. "All wonderful things."

I introduced my mother.

"This is how we do it in France," Sara said, giving my mother two quick pecks on the cheek.

It was a benign enough statement, but I felt as if Sara had slipped a leash over my head and given it a nice tug. A way of reminding me what's at stake here.

"How cultured!" said my mom. Under normal circumstances, this would have embarrassed me but given my deceit, I lacked the capacity for embarrassment. Guilt though, I could do big, heaping mountains of guilt.

I excused myself to the bathroom. On the way, I ran into Gabriela, or rather she materialized in front of me. I felt like a captain who had been thrown overboard by disgruntled sailors. I was mutinied. I was floundering.

"Thank you for coming," I said.

"Thank you for inviting me," she said, even though it had been all Lonely Lou's doing.

"Thank you for thanking me." I was a crazed person.

"Thank you for thanking me for thanking you," she grinned. She had this way of teasing you without coming off as cruel. I loved it and loved being the subject of her attention. I guessed that didn't matter anymore. "Let me buy you a drink," she said, grabbing my arm and guiding me toward the bar.

"The usual," she said when the bartender Biggie finally noticed us. He returned with two Jameson shots and two whiskey gingers. We clinked the shots together and threw them back.

"You know what's crazy? I didn't even realize you and Sara were dating." Gabriela searched my face.

I took a sip to buy some time. "We wanted to keep it hush-hush. Since we work together and all."

"Smart." She turned so her shoulders were no longer facing me. She scanned the bar.

"Sorry I didn't tell you," I said.

"I guess you're a hot commodity," she said, downing half her drink.

I told her I didn't think that was true—I couldn't think of a single other person who was interested in me.

"You're such a fucking bonehead, I swear," she said. Then she whispered, "My favorite fucking bonehead."

Her favorite! It charmed me to think of myself as her favorite anything, even if that did make me a bonehead.

Nearby, someone dropped a glass, the shards flying every which way. "Sorry, sorry, so sorry," said the culprit. I bent down and picked up a large piece, tossing it in the trash can.

"You should let Biggie clean it up. You don't want to cut yourself at your anniversary party," she said, as if cutting myself any other time would be perfectly fine.

I didn't answer. My hands were trembling enough from the tension between us that I had to hold my whiskey ginger with both hands like a toddler. I could see my mom and Sara laughing, her hand resting on Sara's forearm.

"There is such a thing as being too helpful," Gabriela said, looking literally anywhere but at me. It occurred that I couldn't remember a time in which my life had been a product of my own deliberate decisions. What was the word for a buoy without an anchor? Could it still be a buoy if it didn't mark anything?

"I should be getting back." I nodded toward Sara and my mother.

She finished her drink. "Yeah, you should."

Sara didn't give me a sloppy kiss this time but she did throw her arm around my waist in such a casual move I almost forgot we weren't really together.

My mother leaned in close and whisper-shouted in my ear. "I love my daughter-in-law!"

Over the mic, Lonely Lou announced that it was karaoke time. "First up is Sara Bernard! World-famous siren, model, and soon-to-be-wife!"

Sara swaggered toward the stage, partially from drunkenness, partially because that's the way she walked. Shoulders back, chest out, limbs loose and unworried. A full cup of red wine in hand.

Lonely Lou said, "Congratulations to the lovebirds. Equality is so, so great, right? Everyone better buy these two all the drinks they can stomach!"

Inexplicably, she chose to sing "How Will I Know" by Whitney Houston, a song with notes only three people in history can hit. The opening notes played and everyone's heads started bobbing. Sara's singing was way off key, her voice raspy and a little slurred.

"*There's a boy I know, he's the one I dream of...*" She danced a sort of two-step, chugging wine between lines. People were clapping. It was awful.

"*Looks into my eyes, takes me to the clouds above...*"

She even did the *mmm-hmm,* which somehow made the whole experience even worse.

When she reached the chorus, she beckoned me to join her on stage. Everyone turned to look for the lucky lady. Oh, god, I am the lucky lady. When I didn't move, my mom gave me a healthy nudge in the back. I tripped over my toes but caught myself on a sweaty man's back.

Against my will, my feet walked the rest of my body toward the stage. I didn't know how to stop them. Left foot, right, pause for a second behind a swaying woman, then another right around her. I didn't think about where I was going, who I would be when I got there.

"*I'm asking you what you know about these things,*" sang Sara. She'd squatted at the front of the stage, her arm outstretched, hand ready to receive me, ready to ruin me. I could give in to the inevitable. I could give her my hand; I could let that happen. I could run ashore.

I thought instead of Gabriela. I imagine her singing but a reverse siren, every note sending me back out to sea, away from the threats of the island, away from the seduction of destruction. Instead of grabbing Sara's hand, I rip the wine from her fist and dump it down the front of my shirt. A delicious, red mess. She looks shocked but not surprised. I can't explain the difference but I know it has something to do with the fact that the heart doesn't need a body to keep on beating.

It can survive without you.

LAURA McGEHEE

WHAT'S WRONG WITH JANET?

So a scaly reptilian humanoid monster with a color-changing throat kaleidoscopically replaces my long-term lover Janet at breakfast. Sometimes you can catch things before they hit you, like the Frisbee at the office field day in which you masterfully display your physical prowess even though you are a short-term temp and Janet is not yet a long-term lover but rather the exec in that blazer you are trying to impress; but other times, those things hit you in the face, like the holiday football thrown by your mother's second husband Dean who thinks that just because you both sleep with women you'll enjoy tossing prolate spheroids while grunting.

On the morning the reptile comes for me, I wake up to soggy and tangled sheets, the imprint of her body left behind like a crime scene. Everything smells too sweet, as if someone has been baking cookies. I feel clumsily for her body and find a viscous slime so thin it is transparent. I rub my fingers together and feel stickiness. It is not from sex. I have neither entered nor been entered by my long-term lover Janet in weeks. It is not sweat either, which I have been familiar with for upwards of three months—ever since Janet started working out every morning in the gym below her office, making her arms bulge like soup cans under those blazers and her thighs delineate carved muscle, her strong lines made stronger like the coffee she makes too early, too bitter, when everything is still too dark. She receives discounted personal training in that gym. Personally, I would rather train a more practical skill, like becoming an astronaut or cooking an excellent soufflé. Which is what I said when she invited me to join her. Janet says that is my problem, that I will "wait until I'm on fire to jump in the water." However, I think the much more pressing problem is that soufflés cannot rise in space.

She does not ask me to join her in that gym anymore.

My long-term temporary assignment in the office above the gym ended six months ago, anyway.

The transparent trail crosses the carpeting, bending the individual strands over like something heavy has been dragged from the bed. I see I must follow this slimy trail of evidence. I am not the best person for this job but I am the only person. I am only a person and a very average one at that. But if there is anything I have learned from the unexplained phenomenal television that I watch between midnight and two in the morning while Janet snores, it is that even the most regular person can—and should—follow the clues to where they terminate or more likely than not, where someone has been terminated.

Who is more normal than me? I own three pairs of jeans.

I kneel to examine this carpet closely.

I wonder if Janet has been taken from me.

What I know from my viewing of paranormal programs is that if you ever have the opportunity to touch carpet fibers, you do not let that privilege pass by. Anything could be a clue. Best practice is to rub them between your fingers and then smell what you find. I pinch some strands. Crusted and dried. Organic matter? Perhaps. I lift my fingers to my nose. Smells like cookies. Oatmeal? No, chocolate chip. I track the trail out of the bedroom into the kitchen. On the tile the trail becomes slippery. The kitchen is too dark. I sink to my knees and touch each tile in succession to see where the stickiness takes me.

"What are you doing?"

I stop six feet from the kitchen table, where Janet sits hunched away from me, facing the window. The sun is draining the dark from the sky. Her body is formlessly shadowed, a silhouette blacked out like the identity-protected testifiers in *I Was Abducted and My Wife Found Me!*, the show about Midwestern husbands who were abducted by aliens and then their wives found them. Most often naked in an empty cornfield.

"Did you bake cookies?" I ask Janet.

"No." Her voice comes out like melted Chapstick. "It's six in the morning."

"It smells like cookies."

"Are you having a stroke?"

"No," I say, crouching over the kitchen tile, caressing the cheap linoleum with my fingers and sniffing. "I'm just having a good time."

She remains silent, staring out the window, coffee cup serving up steam. Once you start working out before seven in the morning you lose your sense of humor. This is the exchange rate for a very strong body. One of us must stay grounded so right now it is me, so close to the ground while simultaneously prepared at any moment to launch into space just to learn how to whip some egg whites in a small ramekin. This is what my mother calls "give and take" as in "I am giving Dean a vacuum for Christmas so he stops taking me for granted."

Standing up, I try and fail to understand the shape of Janet's bulky shadow. I hear a disgusting sizzling and dripping. Sink must be leaking again? I pour myself some coffee from the French press on the counter and sip. Too bitter, too dark in this room.

"Big day at work?" This demonstrates that I understand the many demands my long-term lover faces as a career-driven woman. I, too, am driven by career—although the car I am driving breaks down for weeks at a time on the side of the highway. This is something my mother would say. So maybe my career is more like piloting a spaceship. I must train for years before my stomach grows strong enough to survive zero-gravity without vomiting. This metaphor is breaking down like the car but space has been on my mind, clearly. A point of contention. Janet thinks the shows I watch while she snores are overproduced and dumb. Entirely fictionalized for entertainment. But I do believe there is life out there. There must be an explanation for all the naked husbands who have been found by all those wives in all those cornfields and I would prefer the most exciting one.

Janet nods. Sips her coffee. All I can see is her shadow and all I can smell are cookies and all I can taste is too-bitter coffee.

"Headed out soon for the gym," she says.

"This early?"

"Meeting Mandy."

"This early?"

She grunts atonal in the same husky way she handles the name of her personal trainer. Mandy. I have not yet met her even though I keep saying we should have her over for dinner. I can try the soufflé recipe my mom sent. Janet says yes definitely but instead I eat lukewarm canned soup while Janet kickboxes past sunset with this heavily tattooed fitness instructor contractually incapable of wearing a shirt over her sports bra.

"Can I turn on the light?" I ask.

She grunts. Turning away, I flip the light switch and her shadow cast by the glow onto the tile is several sizes too large. The cookie smell stuffs itself up my nose and down my throat. It turns into panic and claws its way back up.

Bulging urine-yellow eyes resting inside a long, narrow head tapering into a crackled snout blink at me. The neck stretches accordion-like, teetering above the rest of her crusty human-shaped body layered in thick, multicolor scales that catch light nauseatingly like a kaleidoscope: first a boiling royal purple, then a sea blue, then teal, then forest green, then sunset red. The muscled arms end in sharp, pointed claws grasping the coffee cup. It sits on its haunches on the chair while a long, thick tail paddle-waves absently. It wears my long-term lover Janet's ratty gym t-shirt, arms bulging against the fabric. No pants on bottom. It leaks a yellow, bubbling liquid drip-by-drip from its snout, which falls into the coffee, solving the mystery of the terrible leaky faucet hiss.

"Did you have trouble sleeping?" it asks.

I find it hard to breathe. "A little."

"Up again for a while?"

"A few hours."

"Watching those shows?"

"Yeah."

"That garbage won't help you sleep."

I grunt.

It peers at me. "You doing okay?"

"Just smelling cookies."

"Are you sure you're not having a stroke?"

I feel sick. I feel dizzy. It dismounts the chair and waddles over to me with a large, swinging dinosaur belly and sashaying tail.

"You don't look so well," it says, eyes crusted with accrued yellow gunk, breath reeking of moldy birdcage.

"I'm fine."

It shrugs its bony scaly shoulders. The snout zeroes in on my exposed cheek and plants a slippery lick across my face, my own dear face, scalding the thin hairs on my cheek. I hold my breath.

"Okay. Love you."

"Love you too."

She leaves. I stay.

I am only a person, and not even one who knows how to make a soufflé. Yes, I have never been to space, but I do know someone who knows several someones who probably have, and that is Sher, the host of *I Was Abducted and My Wife Found Me!* She wears dark-wash jeans and a cowboy hat while she stares up at the starry night sky and her own voice narrates, *It's a big, big world up there. This next woman did not give up her search for her husband for over a decade.* I think about what Sher would urge me to do if she were reconstructing my journey through stilted interviews and over-produced B-roll. Shot of a black cat on the fence line. Stock footage of the earth from space. Shot of a hand typing at the computer. *She knew she saw something... inexplicable. She knew she needed to... follow the clues.*

I drink too much coffee and get to work on this investigation. I read too much Kafka until I am nauseated by the metaphor. My situation is the farthest from figurative. So I see what the brightest thinkers have to say in upvoted posts on internet blogs about acute acid trip hallucinations—I did, after all, consume half a Benadryl eight days ago. Three different bloggers describe their mother rescuing them in the end from a dragon, or a flood, or a flood of dragons. Irrelevant. My mother is too busy cleaning to rescue me from anything. I read about extinct lizard species and dinosaurs before checking medieval plague records. I examine so many pustules and none of them look like kaleidoscopic scales.

What choice do I have? Oatmeal? No, chocolate chip?

I need more information. I put on a pair of jeans and follow the creature's residue into the damp day outside. The clouds spit drizzle. The sidewalk is slick. From the rain? Only partially. I kneel and feel the ridged cement, glossy in the center where the creature has slithered. The rain slides off this creature's trail like water on oil so I can follow its path. I look up to the camera that is not watching me and hear Sher's scripted affirmation, her husky voice so soothing. *This wife needed to take the investigation into her own hands if she wanted her husband safely back in his La-Z-Boy ever again.*

I trace the trail towards the office we used to share, back when I was on the long-term temporary assignment that introduced me to my long-term lover whose apartment I moved into when my short-term lease was up at the right time—or the wrong time depending on how you look at it. I don't look at it. I am too busy looking at this trail over these two miles of city sidewalk that have held our lives for two years. Past the small grocery store where I'd buy ingredients for a soufflé if only given the chance. Across the street from the big grocery store where instead I buy the canned soup I have been eating since Janet started missing dinner to kickbox. A right turn at the coffee shop that we used to stop at on our way to work back when I had to borrow her blazers because all the clothes I own have sweat stains.

I am on the street that leads to the gym. Morning rush hour is crowding my progress. My mother calls me. I ignore her call. She calls again. She always knows when I'm up to something.

"Are you up to something?" she asks after I tell her I am busy. Cold mist assaults me. The sound of vacuuming behind her, always the sound of vacuuming.

"No."

"What are you doing?"

"Something."

"So you are up to something."

"It's about Janet."

"It's about Janet, isn't it?"

"Yeah, I just said that."

"I knew it. I could sense it. Can you stop for a minute, Dean?" she yells.

"What?" Dean yells back.

"I'm on the phone! With Val!"

"Oh, hi, Val!"

Still the sound of vacuuming, always the vacuuming.

"Dean says hi."

I push through a throng of suits to find the trail swerving where I knew it would, into the gym below the office we used to share. I can see in through a long stretch of one-way window but the physical specimens moving their fleshy bodies within only see themselves.

"Hi Dean."

"What's wrong with Janet? Did she cut her hair?" my mother asks.

"No."

"Good. She really found the right length for her bone structure."

I observe these bodies testifying to their own humanity: sweat flinging off the brow, thighs tensing and quenching, throats engorging as they gulp water out of paper cones. Nested inside this sea of flesh, sweat, and stink is the scaled impostor in the corner of the gym where the mirrored walls meet and refract endlessly. She stands at the marriage of these two reflections, facing me at the window directly. Beady eyes blank and unfocused as she grunts and heaves two heavy free-weights up above her spindly, towering head. I can see all sides of her through the infinitely mirrored reverberations. The terrible scales flushing red as she pushes. The white underbelly, the tail smacking into each mirrored wall in rhythm with her upward thrusts.

And behind her, straddling that tail, is Mandy.

Wearing only a bra. Her hands on the rough approximation of the creature's hips. I see Mandy nodding, whispering into the creature's ear holes. The creature stares at me with those terrible eyes and I stare back, but I know that it is only seeing itself when it looks at me.

"Are you still there?"

I remember I am on the phone.

"Mom, I need your help with an infestation."

"Oh, no," she says. "You two have bed bugs again?"

"Sort of."

"Roaches?"

"Lizard? I guess."

"Terrible news. How long has it been happening?"

"I can't be sure."

"Okay, honey. Okay. I'll see what I have." Her is voice strained, the vacuum still vacuuming. "Dean! Can you please pause for just one single moment?"

The creature puts down the weights, huffing through its narrow snout. Mandy squeezes the creature's shoulders with both hands. The creature is all pink all over. It turns toward Mandy, and then they are both laughing. Mandy's hands have not left the creature's horrible body.

"Can I come over, now?" I ask.

"I'll get out the tubs from the basement but I'm sorry honey, if you've been having an infestation, I can't let you inside. We just dealt with some mice in the walls. Dean found a dead one on Tuesday by the dog's water. Sucked it right up in the vacuum. Clogged the filter. Had to get a new vacuum. That's the one he's using right now."

"I thought you got him a new one for Christmas."

"I did. This is the second vacuum in two months, can you believe it?"

"I can be there in thirty minutes."

"Great. I'll be done baking these cookies by then."

Even when the trail reached a dead-end, she was not swayed, Sher narrates as I board the train to my mother's house in the suburbs. *At the end of the day, she just really, really wanted her husband home.*

I am now sitting in my mother's backyard on a sunken beach chair too low to the ground, tasteless cookie in my mouth, while she digs through large plastic totes of infestation eradication supplies on the lawn chair across from me. The sound of vacuuming inside. Always. She is wearing latex gloves and a face shield. Her white hair is pulled back so tight her cheek bones protrude. I have eaten four cookies so far with no plan to stop.

"You never should have let it get this bad," she says. "You have to stay on top of infestations else they'll overrun you."

"I didn't realize."

"You know your head is always in the clouds, Val."

"Thank you."

"I don't mean like a pilot. Though that would be a great career for you, by the way, Susie's son Paulo makes six figures flying for United, you know. I'm just glad you've found Janet. Good head on her shoulders—with a great haircut. People need to find their opposites in everything, except cleanliness. That's what being with your father taught me. You need to be exactly the same kind of clean as your partner. But if one of you is out to lunch, the other needs to be making lunch."

She produces an unmarked plastic tub and thumps it on the ground with gravitas. She looks at me with red-veined eyes. "Now, honey, this is filled with a *very* poisonous powder. You find where these lizards are nesting and you flood them with this, okay? And then you need to fill every crack in your home, and listen honey, you want to be doing this consistently every night because it's the only way to ensure *they stay away for good.* I do this regularly and have not had an issue since Dean moved in, as you well know. Except for the mouse that took down a very nice vacuum."

I want to ask about Dean's resemblance to a lizard, if his rail-thin bony aging man body has developed scales, if his neck elongated overnight, if his eyes crust blood-red-yellow when he looks at her.

"How's Dean doing?" I ask, instead.

"Dean? He's fine. I'll make us lunch, soon. He said hello."

"Hi Dean."

"He can't hear you. He's vacuuming."

I take the powder from my mother. She smiles at me joylessly, eyes wrinkled and a brow so creased. "I just want you and Janet to have a clean home. That's all I've ever wanted."

"Me too."

"This will help."

"I hope so."

I take a bag of cookies when I leave. It must be mid-day. I try to hug her with the powder in hand but she holds up her gloved hands toward me, like, *I'm innocent.* She says she cannot risk infecting herself with what I am carrying.

"It's nothing personal," she says. "It's just a very important value that Dean and I both share."

I'm back on the train. Powder in hand.

I'm home. Powder opened.

Smell of cookies overcome by toxic chemical astringency. Thick gloves over my hands, hands into the tub. The powder is chalky and substantive between my fingers. I start to fill the cracks of the home we now share—into the quarter-inch gap between the floorboard and the wall, inside the thick ridges between the cheap tiles in the kitchen, under the door frames where monsters can crawl through.

I reach the bedroom.

I look at the bed.

The imprint of her body still in the crumpled sheets. I hold the rest of the powder over the bed and dump it. I dump all of it. I fill the crime-scene outline that her human form once made. The cloud of chemicals bounces into my nose and I breathe it in, grateful for the scalding and caustic cleansing by this very poisonous powder that promises to rid me of the creature I do not know, the one with arms that are too strong from all the weightlifting, the one whose beady urine-yellow eyes pierce me, how they cut into me, how they cut me apart and slice me open and leave me here, breathing this poison in. It is in my throat. I am coughing. I am feeling better. I am feeling poisoned. I am needing more cookies.

I retreat to the kitchen. Tear open the baggie of cookies from my mother and eat all of them.

Four?

Five?

Oatmeal?

No, chocolate chip. They taste like nothing. They chalk in my mouth with the poison cloud. Tears grow out of my eyes but not due to sadness. I am triumphant. I have followed the clues and secured the home and locked the doors. Sher somewhere is wearing her surest jeans, she is sitting across from the blacked-out shadow of the wife who followed the trail where it led, and Sher is saying, *What you did was tremendous*, and Sher is saying, *He would have died of exposure, naked in that field, if you hadn't kept looking.*

So I can breathe easy, by which I mean choking on a very poisonous powder. Maybe this is training for space, where you do not even have the luxury of poisonous air. Up there you cannot breathe so down here on the ground where I am grounded, I should feel lucky, I should feel grateful. Every partnership needs contrast and maybe tonight I'll finally make that soufflé. This is called self-care.

Tonight, the creature who used to be my long-term lover Janet will return and this poison will salt her like a snail. Shriveled, she will shrink and fit in the palm of my hand and I will flush her down the toilet. Finally I will eat my dinner in peace.

I will keep the cracks in my apartment dusted. Where my long-term lover went, I cannot follow. Which is into a gym. And I will never join a gym, not when there is so much space to conquer. I am only a person and for this I should be grateful. Not everybody has this luxury. When Sher asks, *Please, let me and the viewers at home know— at the end of everything you've been through—do you believe there's life out there?*

I will answer no. I do not believe there is life in here. Not after this poison. Not anymore.

FRANKLIN K.R. CLINE WALKS INTO A BAR

i know i know the book ends
with me walking out of a bar
and never so far walking back in falling
in love with olivia in good health

to have a happy ending as though endings
are happy as though endings
mean a real ending as though i have the gall
to say i know what it means to end

i know what it means to end i think for now although
the ending is ongoing it is powered
by love once i read a cliche that had a poem in it

its cold outside -9 degrees the streets are freezed
a still image of frozen glop that on 34 degree wednesday will melt
into dirty water

FRANKLIN K.R. CLINE

FRANKLIN K.R. CLINE WALKS INTO A BAR

for klingers east

and it kicks ass! bars rule
cant swing my dick without hitting a bar in milwaukee

love to sit on a stool and find franklin k.r. cline
chatting with whoever amongst

the brewers game
the crossword in todays paper

passed around. who got
this next round? ah,

thanks. i got the next one
four five six of us sittin around

each buys two rounds im no
mathematician but thats eight drinks

amongst the four five six of us in an hour snow falls
and we stumble home showered in it

FRANKLIN K.R. CLINE

FRANKLIN K.R. CLINE WALKS INTO A BAR

with a line from the young rascals

ah everyone digging it having fun we are full of and
out of love and groovin

on a sunday afternoon the cool bar
next to the acupuncture place

have a few and maybe a shot
or two with the bartender who doesnt

know the depths of your addiction! whoa
this shit is gonna kill you dude

this shit is gonna kill you dude
your veins will be so visible

your body is an unwatered plant but
you are not a cactus man you cant

just live this kind of wet life drink water
remember nmi wiconi

TOM ROTH

MASON JAR

THAT SUMMER, a few weeks after we buried Dad, Ross trapped a cardinal in the Mason jar. He messed with me about that bird until I almost wept like a little sister was supposed to. Standing at the top of the sun-beaten steel slide, he raised the jar to the burning light. Shook it. The cardinal fluttered inside the glass.

"Don't!" I yelled up at Ross.

"I'm older than you."

"That's bullshit," I argued. Everyone had started cussing after sixth grade but with little Danny around, I tried not to. It was hard, though, because of Ross. Stood as a broad freshman. Behaved like a deranged first grader. "Just cause you're older, you don't get to—" The cardinal cocked his head and cried in the jar. "You're hurting him!"

Danny squatted on the bottom edge of the slide, glued to my old yellow Nintendo Game Boy. I gave the video game to him since Mom couldn't afford the new one. She worked overnight at a convenient store. Slept through the summer days. Almost invisible. Left me to look after Danny and protect him from Ross.

Danny needed big dorky glasses right after the funeral. Said he saw Dad in the cornfield with them on. A boy's weird way of dealing with death, I figured. Or maybe he was losing it like Ross. Maybe we all were.

"Knock-knock," Ross teased, rapping his knuckle against the jar.

Dad limped on fresh cut grass. Carrying the jar, he struggled into the reeds, vanishing. Frogs croaked from the flatland of soggy woods. A cool evening in late May. Purple sky over the darkened trees. Some red from the sunset remained above the cornfield on the other side of the road. Fireflies glowed in the high grasses and reeds at the edge of our backyard. Ross roasted marshmallows and hot dogs over the bonfire. Danny tapped his video game, squinting.

"You need glasses," Mom said to him, tousling his hair.

"Mallow or dog, Jess?" Ross asked.

"Both."

"Atta girl," Mom said.

We braided our dark hair. Mine a thick rope of knots, hers a tight sleek fishtail. Ross and Danny helped Dad gather the sticks and logs for the fire while we braided. Mom had to start over on mine because I got up when Dad built the pyramid. I handed him the kindling, then told him sit down and tell us where to place things. He fell off a roof one day at work and never recovered, arms and legs like the twigs Danny handed me. Dad was the only one with glasses then.

"Where is he?" Mom said, looking back.

She called his name. Fireflies flashed near the reeds. Yellow-green specks floated and faded, floated and faded, slower than the ones Dad cupped in his hands to show me when I was Danny's age, the bright bug in his palms, then in mine. No answer.

"Jess," Mom said, "go see if he's okay back there."

"Why can't Danny go?" I said.

"Danny's helping with the food," Ross said. He blew out a fiery marshmallow. "Check on him, Jess."

I remembered his dark eyes in the firelight. Soft and warm. Bright with dancing flames. Fixed on a charred marshmallow.

"You're killing him, Ross!"

July was suffocation. Trees wavered in the warped thickness of heat and humidity. My moist skin felt coated. Smothered by a sticky layer of invisible mud. Ross wrapped his red shirt around his head to make a bandana. The pasty skin of his torso glimmered in the harsh sunlight. I was reminded of Dad's pale face in the coffin. His dead expression. Tired and hurt. In pain. Danny wiped drops of sweat off his video game with his Pokémon shirt.

"Danny, do girls know how knock-knock jokes work?" Ross asked.

Danny let out a nervous laugh before lowering his head. The cardinal flapped and flapped against the jar. Wanting to fly. Cicadas trilled and buzzed. Long branches reached over the mossy roof of our narrow house. Birds rose into a V and soared in the direction of the cornfield. The cardinal banged against the glass wall of the jar, singing for sky and trees and air. His red wings fluttered and folded, fluttered and folded, in failure of flight.

"Goddammit, Ross." Danny squinted when he heard me, more afraid of my voice than the word. I sounded like Ross. "Just let him go. All he wants to do is fly."

"I don't give a flying fuck." Danny looked up again. "What difference does it make anyway? The bird's gonna die at some point."

Ross knocked his knuckles against the jar. The cardinal shuddered and cried.

"You're sick."

In those months after Dad's death, I watched Ross spiral into a strange distortion of grief. Stole money from Mom. Stole the jar from my room. Stole disgusting shit from the movie store in town. Watched hours of sex in his room. I could hear all of it in mine. I barged in once to throw a book at him. Instead I found Danny by himself. Frozen in confused terror. Naked people on the screen. Maybe Dad saw what became of Ross, of all of us. I thought of him limping behind the reeds somewhere.

"Alright, alright," Ross laughed. "All you have to do is answer the joke and I'll let this little bitch go."

I glanced at the jar. Then at Danny, who waited for my answer.

"Who's there?"

I pushed through the wall of reeds. Their feathered tops shed onto my shoulders as I pressed between thorny bushes. Fireflies illuminated the deep expanse of tangled thickets of shrubs and ivy. Discovery of a second world. Darkness flashing with stars of green light.

"Dad," I called through the forest.

Far back in the woods, I spotted him in a small glade near the creek beneath the blinking lights. Slumped against a large rock on the ground, he bowed his face over his lap. A strong light was in his hands as if he had plucked a green star from the sky.

"Dad," I called again.

Earlier that day, I had my first one. I rushed to the upstairs bathroom and bled into the clear toilet water. I knew what was happening. Still freaked me out. Dad stopped me in the hallway with his hand on my shoulder when I came out.

"You look like you just saw a ghost," he said. His hand trembled. "You okay?"

"I'm fine," I replied.

"Dad," I said in the woods. He didn't move. I picked up my pace, splashing in the creek and over the damp floor of the dark green world I had discovered behind the reeds.

"Dad!"

I could never tell with Ross's eyes. Dark blue marbles. Same as Mom's. I prayed those eyes might fall out and roll down the slide and land in the dirt. I'd wash them under the faucet. Study them with a magnifying glass.

"Who's there?" I asked again.

"Norway."

"Norway who?"

"Norway you're getting this fucking jar!"

Ross stomped down the slide, shoved Danny, and sprinted around the house with the jar.

"My game!" Danny cried. He picked up the yellow console and showed me the screen. "It's cracked!"

"It's fine," I said. "Look. See? You can still play it." I picked up his glasses and cleaned the oblong lenses with my shirt. "Here. It'll be okay. Come on."

Danny and I hurried around the juniper bushes to find Ross on the other side of the street. He stood before the green cornfield. Heat rolled off the pavement. I hoped his marble eyes might pop out. He'd feel for them on the hot road until an Amish buggy crushed him. He pounded his chest with his fist a few times before disappearing into the cornfield.

"Wait here."

"Just tell on him, Jessica," Danny whined. "Don't leave. You won't find him. Ross knows everything about the cornfield."

"No, he doesn't." The cornfield never belonged to us. We sometimes snuck in and played there even though we weren't supposed to. "Don't listen to all those things he says about ghosts and murderers and giant snakes. It's just a cornfield."

"Please just tell on him first."

Above us, a high droning rose and drowned out the cicadas. Far in the sky, a plane circled past the trees surrounding the farmland.

"Oh shit." I grabbed Danny's hand and rushed inside to wake up Mom. "Come on!"

"Dad! Dad! Dad!"

I sprinted across the shallow creek and shook his shoulders. His head fell back on the rock. Mouth agape. Eyes shut. I screamed for Mom. A chorus of frogs sang. The creek flowed over stones and twigs.

In his dead hands beamed the jar, full of fireflies and gathered light. I looked at him and waited for his eyes to open.

A crane fly landed on his forehead.

"Go stand with your brother!" Mom said after she turned around in the road. Her hair was frizzy and wild, like she tossed and turned in a haunted sleep. I wanted to wash her head and braid a fishtail.

"Mom—"

"You shut your mouth and do what I say, Jessica!"

"Fuck you," I said, low enough she couldn't hear it.

She disappeared into the cornfield. I hustled back to Danny. He was looking through the binoculars he had taken from Dad's desk when we went inside. Dad got into bird watching after his fall. He said it eased him. Finding birds took his mind off the pain.

After completing its circle, the plane flew over the distant silos again, heading our way. The cornfield rose high like a great green wave with the farmhouse and silos upon the faraway crest.

"You see them?" I asked.

Danny shook his head. "Can you melt to death if that spray gets on you?"

"No. It's bad for you, but you won't melt."

"But Ross said that—"

"Ross is full of crap, Danny." He glanced up at me, confused. "He's a liar. Don't listen to him." He peered through the binoculars again. "Give me those for a sec."

"Wait," he whispered. "I see him."

"Does Ross have the jar?"

"No, no. It's Dad. I see him. He has a smile." Danny gasped, then smiled beneath the binoculars. "Now he's waving." He waved his hand at the cornfield. "He sees me."

"Danny, please, not now," I said.

With a loud roar, the plane descended. White spray in the sky. A ghost over the cornfield. Mom ran out with the empty jar in her hands. The spray spread into a mist behind her.

"It's okay," she coughed. She held the jar like a football player. Her other arm wrapped over Danny's shoulders. "It's okay."

"Is Ross alive?" Danny asked.

"I know where he is," Mom said.

Back inside the house, Ross waited in Dad's chair at the kitchen table. He wore his red shirt now. Sweat dripped down his forehead. His hair tangled into black flames.

"She saved him!" I yelled. "Mom saved the cardinal!" I took the empty jar and held it above my head.

"So what if she did." Ross stared out the window. His eyes followed the plane in the sky. He spoke softly, his voice weak and choked up, faltering. "You think I give a fuck about a bird? It's gonna die anyway. Like the rest of us."

"Enough!" Mom ordered. "Waking me up for this nonsense. You," she said to Ross. "In my room now. Who do you think you are?"

I walked away, pissed off, carrying the Mason jar. I stopped Danny in the hallway upstairs. The binoculars were still on his neck.

"Did you see the cardinal fly out of the cornfield?"

"I don't know. I saw Mom running out with the jar." Danny sat down at the top of the stairs. Before I went into my room, he said, "But I really did see him, Jess. I saw Dad in the cornfield. He waved at me."

"Danny, stop it."

"It was him."

"I said stop."

The jar fell out of my hands and rolled on the carpet. I walked into my room and collapsed on my bed and thought about praying. My sweat dampened the sheets. I didn't know what to pray for. I just kept saying God, please. Please, God. Please. Please.

I grabbed the scissors on my nightstand. I held my breath for a long time. I dragged the closed blades beneath my shirt. I opened them and pressed the cold edge into the skin of my collar bone and breathed on the pillow. I pressed harder. I stopped praying to God and spoke to the cardinal instead. I know she saved you. I know you're alive. I know you're flying.

"Jess."

My heart jumped. I slid the scissors under the pillow.

"Jess."

I wiped the tears from my cheeks and rolled over. It was Danny. He stood in the doorway, iridescent, gazing down the hall, his finger pointed at the flashing floor and his glasses glowing with a soft reflection of emerald light.

"He's here."

ZAKIYYAH DZUKOGI

BLISS IN BOTTLE

on days
night glides down
in sun,
the air crooks in winter,
the cloud crams our space,
till a chick grows a tooth.
on nights
the tongue in our mouths
thaws like a botched-up pastry,
that, that fills our noses
slips in the shawl
of a baked fire.
once beside a stream
in our bodies,
a full drub
loosed its lips
in our numbed ears.
we weaved words
in the pale evenings
of a blended song
and bleached our nights,
our floor tiled
in gingered diamonds,
our bliss in bottle.

CHARTS, PRIMARY

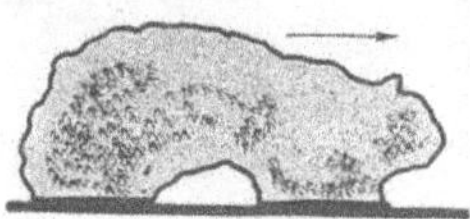

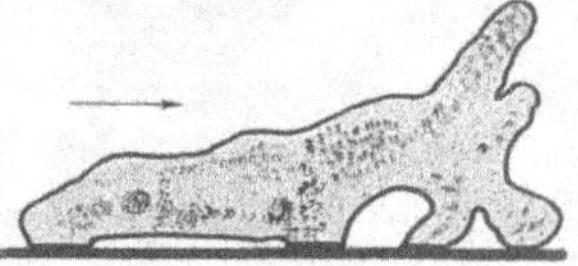

Organoconceptual Mesomorphism Pseudo-Evolution Exhibiting Perpetual Inertial Ineptitude; this powers Old Oaty's internal coordination & fragrance saturation motors

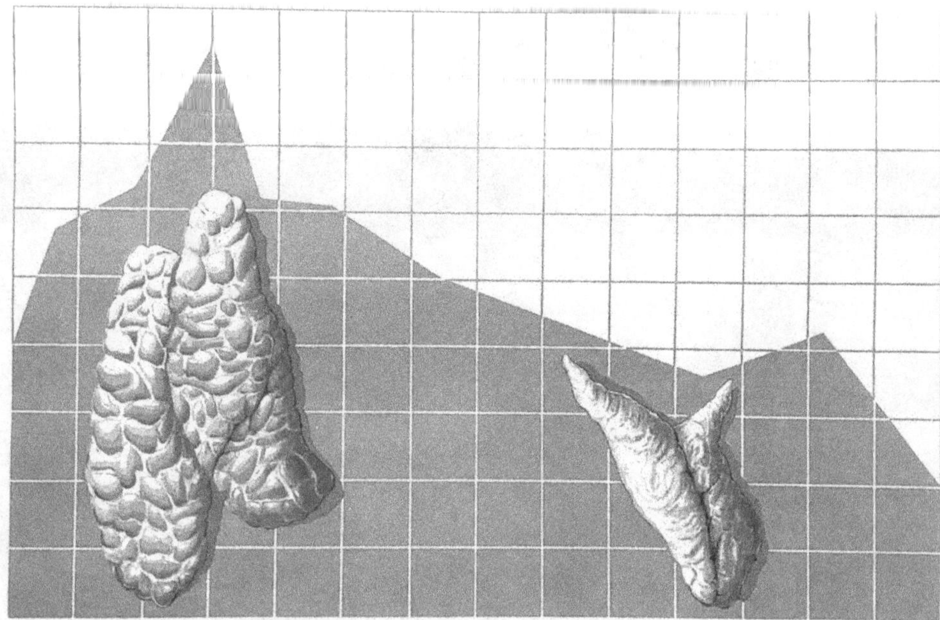

Comparison of Primary Expectations with Eternal Outcome Showing Overall Decline in Output and Complexity and General Increase in Hypercasual Defulpulation

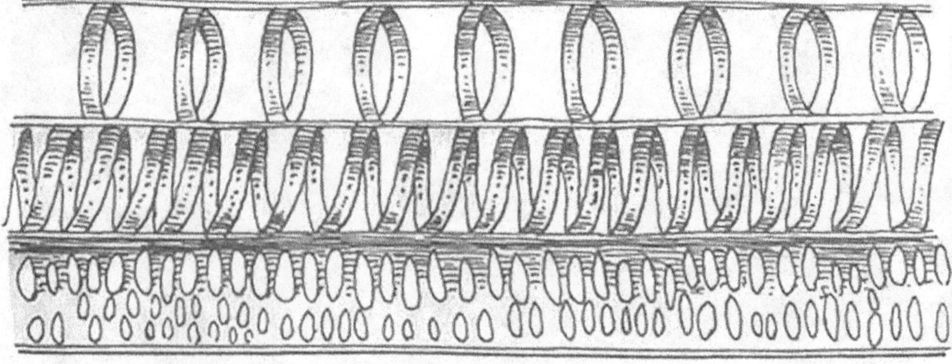

Interaxial Rendering of Cosmic Transit Patterns Extrapolated Superconsciously into a Non-Dimensional Space, Including 12th-Level Sensory Oblongations

SORAMIMI HANAREJIMA

MODERN COGNITION

She has been sullen for days on end and I can't stand to see her like this—so unlike herself, utterly demoralized by the recent accomplishments of her peers as if they've declared a referendum on her abilities. Her sense of self-worth shouldn't be so debilitated by the success of others. It's unbecoming and unhealthy.

So I make her a social comparison blocker: custom-crafted cognitech packed into a hair clip, an alligator-style barrette that she can easily wear as an unobtrusive accessory to constantly, preemptively inhibit her mind's habit of benchmarking herself against others. Once it's done, I meet her in the rose garden to hand off the hair clip. Reticent with despondency, she simply accepts the glossy blue barrette with what muted appreciation she can muster, then uses it to hold back a lock of hair she usually tucks behind her ear. I watch intently as her mood improves in mere seconds; she perks up, eyes wide, poise regained—like she's fully awake now with a lucidity that brightens the already luminous swath of flowering shrubs behind her.

Delighted by this transformation, she keeps the clip in her hair all throughout the following days, perched above her left ear, an ornamental good luck charm she's unwilling to risk being without. Thanks to the cognitive noise cancelation the blocker provides, she soon becomes more than just self-assured, turning unequivocally breezy—to the degree that she blows off work responsibilities and embarks on an impromptu tropical getaway.

Her sudden departure leaves me with the impression that she didn't really care about making her mark in the field of chronopsychography. Which leads me to think that through their negation, I've revealed her fervent ambitions as being ultimately rooted in the desire to outdo colleagues in her discipline—the manifestation of a competitive streak the social comparison blocker has obliterated.

The following week, I receive a postcard from her. A picture of a lush cove with a rocky waterfall nestled amid palm trees, with only a large smiley face and my address in blue pen on the back.

Is she going to be nonchalant toward everything now? Maybe I need to make a new hair clip that includes a passion amplifier, to get her in touch with deeper motivations. And a focus enhancer also, if I can fit one in. A few hours later, I'm prototyping in earnest, seeing how many bells and whistles I can cram together.

Finally, she returns after weeks spent on sun-drenched beaches and sultry sea cliffs. I meet her for coffee, ready to stage another intervention. But before I can venture into further cognitive modification, she slides a manuscript across the café table towards me. Its bold title seems to stare up at me from the tabletop.

WHAT CONSCIOUSNESS IS FOR

I flip over the cover page to find a single line of centered text that dedicates this work to me. Just me.

"Couldn't have done it without you," she says, her words melodious with glee.

Scanning through the abstract on the following page, I learn that what lies before me is a treatise on the nature—if not the very purpose—of consciousness as a means of expanding causal power, augmenting agency by putting deliberative distance between stimulus and response.

"Wow," I murmur.

"It's amazing what sunny days by the ocean will get you thinking about when you have a clear mind," she says, as though relaying a message from a part of herself that lingers on in those days.

"You think that's what consciousness is really for?" I ask.

"Yes. To riff off Steven Pinker, consciousness was the real innovation in our biological evolution. Everything since has just made our thoughts travel farther or last longer."

Then what about our technological evolution? Is cognitech also making our thoughts travel farther or last longer? And if so, how far can they go? How far will they take her?

But I mention nothing of these questions, expecting her to say more, even bring up ideas related to them. Instead, she turns to the wide pane of window beside us, casting her gaze skyward, as though it will arc over the low clouds and into the distance, toward some faraway destination. Still her constant companion, the barrette glints with afternoon sunlight. And I become uncertain whether next time she will return and tell me about her thoughts. But how much does should that matter?

"I'll be right back," I murmur.

In the restroom, I remove one of the new barrettes from my pocket. I run the tip of my index finger over its surface four times, back and forth over the same shiny blue coating as the one she's wearing. Pressing it to my forehead, I close my eyes and wait for the brief buzz that tells me it's in recording mode. When it trembles against my skin, I focus on the kind of presence she's been in my life: that reassuring warmth even when she's not around—as though the yellow from the flickering candle was her in the alpine hotel's reading room during that off-season evening. Once I'm done, I set the replay strength and frequency of my recording to quiet and sporadic. Just a light reminder. Just in case. Then, for good measure, I make the necessary adjustments to the other barrettes, recalibrating the discretion of the autonomous modulators—the loop breaker, obsession mitigator, inner voice filters, self-image stabilizer, social validation emulator.

When I return to my seat, I lay out the retuned barrettes on the table, in the space between her coffee cup and monograph on human cognition. I can feel her gaze following my hand as I place these hair clips end to end, forming a line.

"I made a few more for you," I tell her. "Now you'll have a couple matching pairs. And when you feel like livening things up, you can wear the red ones."

FICTION

"Those have a nice pop to them."

"I think so too."

"Thanks, I love them already."

I look at these things on the tabletop, that we've brought for each other as though we had agreed to meet here for an exchange of bespoke gifts. Crisp, white paper with sharp, black letters. Smooth, colorful plastic encasing tiny circuitry. Ideas that once only existed in our minds made physical to exist in the gulf between them. Souvenirs we'll each have of this coffee date—of one another.

I lift my gaze, seeking out her eyes with mine, to look into them just because I can, just because she and I are still here, just because we are close enough to do that for a while.

KYLE E MILLER

UNTITLED[I]

She disappeared on a painted mare
Hunting for morels the size of children's brains
Far too late in the season of the last Bealtaine.
The midnight druid captured the dogs sent to search
But the hunters found the mare's bones buried
2,000 years ago beside a lost draft of *Metamorphoses*.

A ram capering among the scheming ewes
Like Eros in an autonomous zone.

Strength is stepping on an ant without crushing him.

The men who believe music sounds a certain way
Stand in a forest of rifles talking about
Young girls as if they were horses and
Climbing the lips of God with mud on their feet.

The difference between here and there being that
Here the word for world is unspoken.

KYLE E MILLER

UNTITLED[II]

Clouds the color of veins as a storm
Rearranges the attic of the sky.
Old memories tumble from sealed boxes.
Fault lines shift in the earthen cellar.
A claustrophobic, gauzy Sunday
Like mounting a horse underwater.
My mind, a pudding; I hate children
And dogs, but only when they speak.

I expose the genitals of a pole bean blossom:
Three whip-tailed insects squirming,
Declaring, I think, their disgust for the light.

In practice, language becomes like the nearly
Infinite arrangements of features on the
Faces of humanity: if they were all the same we
Might learn the meaning of a curled lip
But as it stands, we know nothing.

Expression is best, that is, most beautiful, when
Silent, capacious, open in the manner of
Constellations, because those who tell me to
Love everyone seem to hate humanity the most.

Ideas appear to sculpt the circus of history,
But in the end you have only a pair of
Jacob's shoes and nowhere to place them.

Certainly not on his feet.

KYLE E MILLER

UNTITLED[III]

The secret is to stop flinching.

The mosquito bite returns each evening at the
Hour of its creation seven days ago, a Sunday.
It doesn't itch, only rises like evidence of a new bone.
Hate is an iron rod in a rainstorm: its rust
Poisons the strawberries beneath, flour white
Blossoms turn orange, and the fruit dries up
In the mouth of the last month of summer.

I'm just a clay boy sculpted in the shallows
As the mountain shapes moisture into rivers.

Flies are named for the teeth of other animals -
I would rather be bitten by a deer than a horse.
A new trail is a loaf of bread, a skin of water,
The melon of good and evil, which is to say,
Everything. Meteor shower of frogs at my feet,
And a dragonfly of prehistoric size.

Words are a way of remaining alive: they fall in a
Predetermined order from the childhood of time.

How can I possibly remain present when the smell of
Ripe strawberries ambushes me in the parking lot
Beside the unexplored meadow? If you had drilled
A hole in my head ten years ago and sent a worm
Inside with your eyes, this is what it would have seen.
Not a thought in sight. How does he stay in motion?

But one day, he finds some thoughts that need thinking.

Birds require at least 497 acres of air to be happy.
A card at the kiosk offers to send me images of cranes,
And to my surprise the 9-million-year-old fossilized
Wing of a sandhill crane arrives six weeks later.
The bone leaps from the bubble wrap and fuses
With my left scapula; I may never reach the ceiling,
But at least from here I can see where I used to be.

I am the quiet thought you return to when all the loud ones have
gone away.

LODGING

MIGRATORY CLOSET

Our most modestly-priced accomodations, migratory closets are an affordable and fun way to travel. You'll never be able to guess where your closet is tomorrow!

ESSENCE VIAL, BUCKET, OR VAT

Ideal for our gaseous and liquid guests, we offer these accommodations at varied volumes. Ask about our Vat with a View Upgrade!

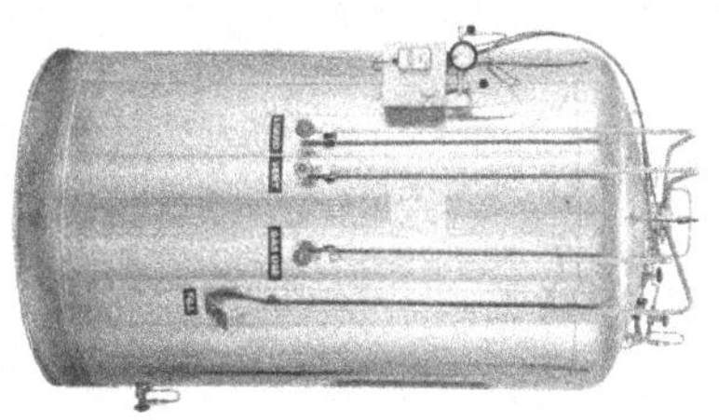

CRYOCART®

Lose yourself for an eternity (or two!) in our plush, completely and totally reliable cryopreservation facilities. Save on our family-sized cryotanks.

ROLLED UP NEWSPAPER IN A SEPTIC TANK

Snuggle up with the finest parchment from atop Mont Eepithon, immersed in a rich, foamy bath of pure feculence, hand-strained by our dedicated team.

RIDICULOUSLY GARGANTUAN SUITE

You'll be astounded by how much space we can fit into space! Is it impossible for a space this large to exist inside a train? You bet it is!

GREG'S ROOM

Just the way he left it, perfectly preserved, eternally unperturbable. In Greg's words: "What would it be like to sleep having never been awake?"

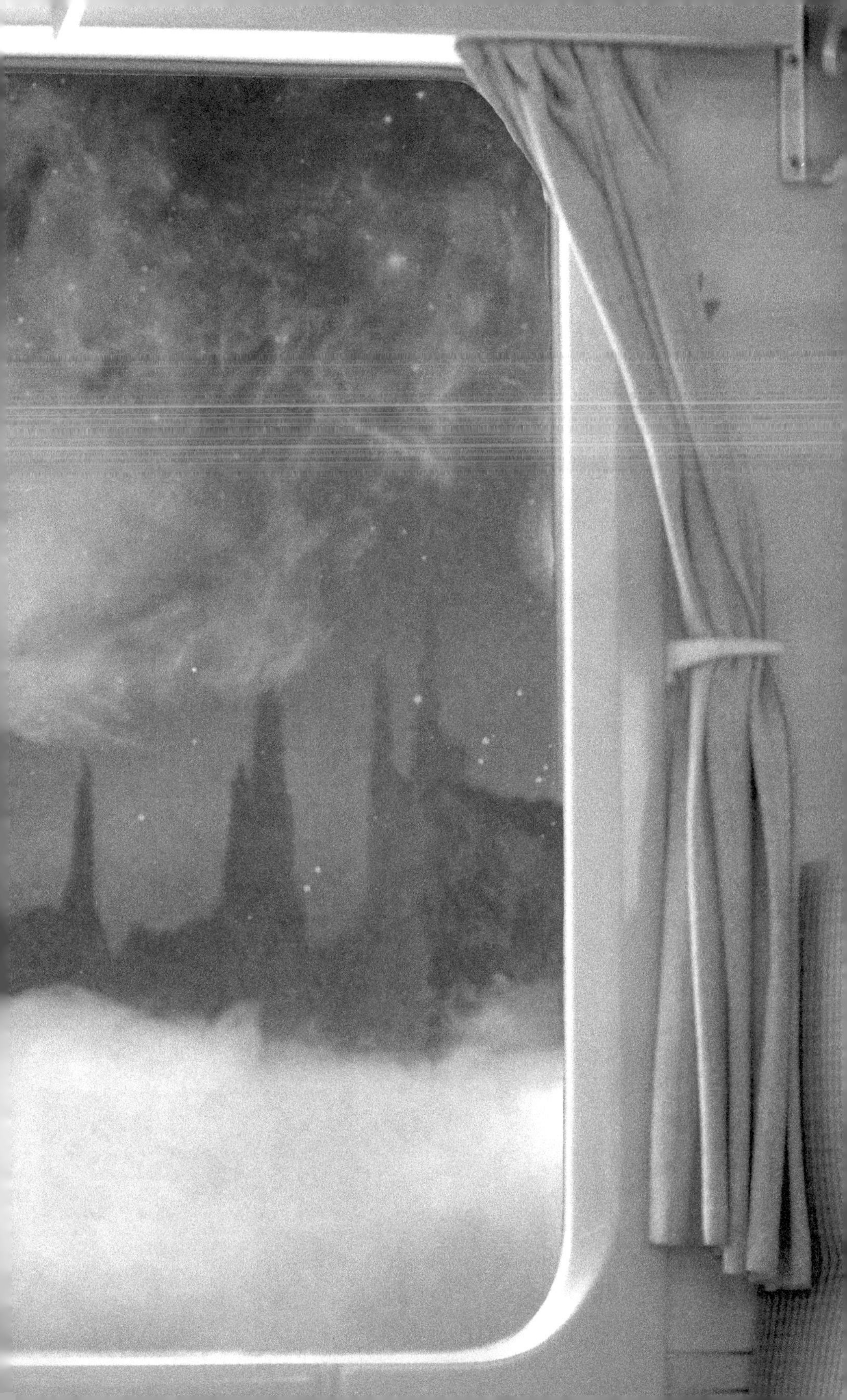

CURRENT CONDITIONS AT THE SUMMIT

DANIEL GALEF

IN YON BLACK STRUGGLE YOU COULD NEVER KNOW ME

O Drearysome day, gunny-grey and rain not drops but a fine diffuse haze. Bus window is the emergency one, red handle Pull it! Pull it! That would be a fun, a sight, if I rattled someone so he tipped back into road river Splash!

Then.

Vict.

The spect arrives no sheet, no ectoplasm and wrapped not in chain but slick black raincoat. He's standing at busfront stiff as a hard-on and white as a bleached femur, his suit is printed in the *Illustrated New Cyclopedia* under the word "suit" and also under the word "square." So ghost he ain't, he died but I am deader, he once undid but I am a more undoer.

We were a pair, we were not even a pair we were a one, "inseparable" what they call companions so fast, as lightning. We struck twice. I knew him through ages before we knew we were young, grit-grimacing sandbox summers and a camp with an Indian name where we became blood brothers under a rite we invented.

Our eye-beams are touching, but there is no arc. Vict doesn't recognize me, I can tell. I cognize him one because he is so changed. I saw then his shoulders eroded sixteen springs and also his wings shorn and his eye was spintry. Never saw I such a spintry one as that Vict's eye. I made. If he won't connect me I can lever, or if he'll know he know but not how or who.

Some people assume I am homeless, an acceptable explanation to justify my patchworks, my lack of seams. In fact this is because I have torn out all tags, markings. Through this unseamliness I make myself noone. How much noone? Now I can test. To fool him so close like to fool myself, to hide myself from the searching eye of myself, game of hunt-the-thimble where I am hider and hunter and also thimble.

Heck-o! I cry. Hale! What devil emptied you on our green globule! But he is practiced watching ahead like to death, hearing things unremembered and not me in front of him here could be anyone. I pluck at him with magic. Victor! I hue, piercing, punctual. Where are your spoils? Have you written my histories?

(That names are formule ancient croaking spirit-mumblers knew this. (Mine is Jims, I fear not tell you.))

Vikki-vikki-vikki-vikki—!

This has gotten him. Knocked off his gutwagon he squinced, knew then he knew me but couldn't figure how and finally admitted. Who are you thing? How have you figured me? Did we walk in a dream?

Here I mighted gun YES dummkopf and spell out our histories which he has not writ but the delicious shock of him was already annoying. A thimble is something in the shape of a human part but hardened. NO!, I say instead spittle to his nosel a little bit, You could be anyone but I know these hiddens anyway. Here is your Chinese zodiac animal and here is your favorite brand of breakfast cereal.

He is reeling but not recognizing. I feel a prick. What am I a thimble for? My needle should not poke me.

My eye has become spintry. How can he still not get? Am I that good? I cannot be noone, not really. Think. I am no some things, no Vict, no prosopragnosticator. But I am no nobody truly. I am no backwards Omen. Is he pretending? Is he me-ing? What if he is not even Vict? Friend or faux, how could he be he, and not know? Like a foundering, I list—

I know your birthday Brontë's and I know the color of your childhood dogs which was red and black and yellow and black. I know your technicolor guitar fancies and also I know your buriedest and most destroying secrets which I will shout out now on this bus. And I gulp a big breath of air. But I am waiting for Vict to sing first, waiting for him to say the word that will speak me into existence and destroy me.

SATOSHI IWAI

SAILING AWAY

From morning till night, even while sleeping in the bed, the old man is always wearing a sailor suit, although he is not and has never been a sailor. His dementia is getting worse day by day. Of course he doesn't notice it. The crows are perching on the TV side by side. He doesn't notice it too.

The old man chops pineapples in the kitchen. He believes that the name of new Eden is hidden in a pineapple, so he chops dozens of pineapples every day. The kitchen is filled with the smell of rotten fruits. Whenever he buys new pineapples, the greengrocer gives him a puzzled smile.

Every night the old man roams around the town. He takes different routes each time, but when looking down from the moon, all of them show the contours of various ships. In his brain, his blood flows as slowly as a large river. It will reach the ocean before long.

SATOSHI IWAI

HALLEY'S FLOWER

In November, the shadows of the street trees grow thinner day by day. The face of the daytime moon looks wearier hour by hour. I feel as if I had an uncle who had traveled all around the world. He often told me about his love affairs with a lot of women. One day, he headed for somewhere to find the hottest love on earth and never came back. All he left in his apartment is a tiny pot in which a flower bud is about to open. I take the pot to the flower shop on the dark, empty street, and ask an old clerk what kind of plant it is. Standing by the dark, empty showcase, she tells me that it is the loneliest pistillate flower on earth that blooms only once in seventy-six years. When the clerk turns her face toward me, I notice that she is totally blind. Her eyes are as hollow as the daytime moon. I feel as if I could hear a lullaby for all bees which are mortal in November.

SATOSHI IWAI

FLYING CHEF

He is a flying chef who works for a flying restaurant. Every day he cooks for the banished angels who are on the way to the sinful earth, so he has been busy recently. When he washes the dishes with the midnight rain and wipes them with the silky clouds, the stars start twinkling for him.

His specialty is fried pigeon, fried flying pigeon to be exact. He uses knives and tongs so quickly that the birds never perceive themselves being chopped while flying. Even after soaked in hot oil, they are still flying in rows of sliced meat. The waiter carries them on his arm like a handler.

The chef's fiancée, staying on the earth, waters a pea plant every night. When the beanstalk reaches the moon, they will go on their honeymoon. They already have a little son who has slimy wings on his back. He makes a practice of chopping sparrows every afternoon.

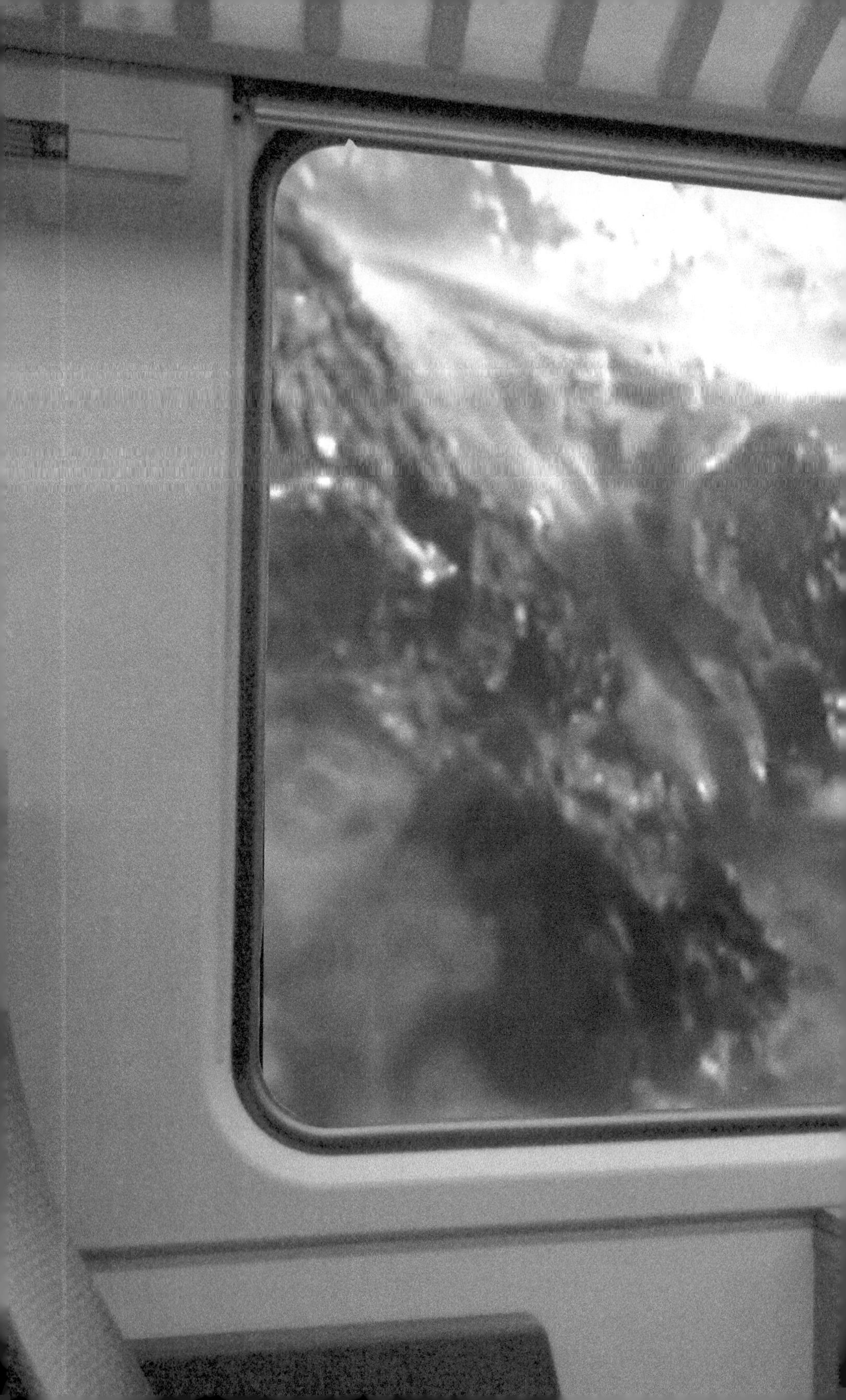

MEET THE TEAM

GRUNTHILDA, 1ST-CLASS ENGINE

Does a lot of the work. Most of the work, really. Everyone else is kind of a hanger-on.

THANDOR KOR BOGLOR

Carries ore, no more. Some say that's a bore, but we're sure there's lots to adore.

MONTESFORTH ABERSHIRE

Has two parts, each carries different things. But sometimes the same thing. It's 50/50, really.

CHARTREUSE QUILN

Carefully stores the ever-slumbering consciousnesses of the drifting incorporeal terror-hordes of Bontrex 3784.

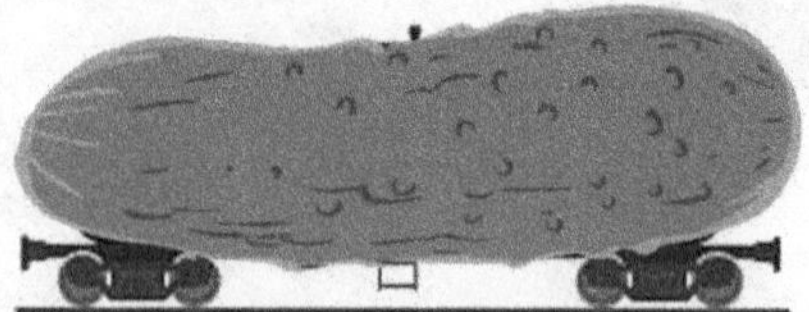

Q-CAMBER OF PLANET VYNE-GARR

Possessed by multiple levels of sentience, this car is a real snappy treat for the senses. We recommend visiting during the Sand Wedge stretch of the journey.

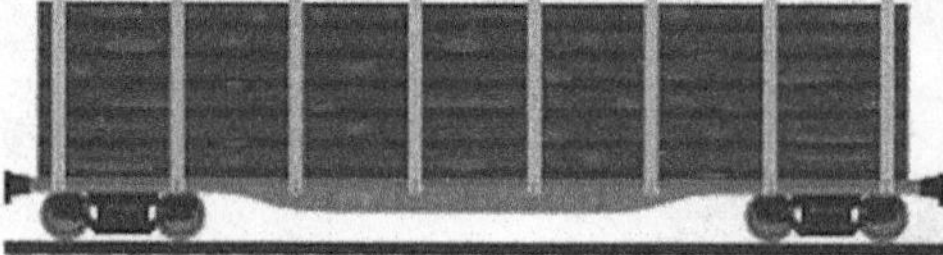

BERT

Please do not ask about Bert. Please. We beg of you. Nothing good can come from asking, or even thinking, about Bert.

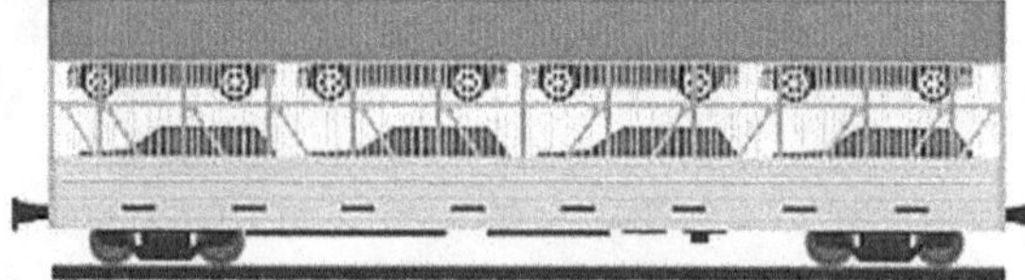

HOPPLEBERRY SWIFT IV

Automobile, flying saucer, moonbuggy, solar monowheel, and cosmic go-kart carrier extraordinaire.

SHORT (THE SHORTEST) LAMMY

Contains the gateway to the 97th long (the longest) dimension of lost socks. Do not enter if you are aware of socks.

SAMUEL ZAGULA

A TOASTER

My toaster is a liar. I entrust it with the items that I need for the continuation of my existence and it betrays me. It changes the time it takes to toast. I suspect it has a deep hatred towards me because I am conscious and it is not. That's probably why it changes the time it takes to make my toast. I select "Five" on the button of the toaster that dictates time. It does not give me five pieces of time. Once it took four minutes and thirty-two seconds; another time it took five minutes and five seconds. I require consistency. Without consistency, the atoms that make up this world wouldn't know how to grab on to each other and everything would fall apart.

I ask my friend to come over and help me. He collects his fingernail clippings in tiny plastic bags and makes dolls out of them. He numbers his dolls with a black Sharpie, so he won't forget. He's just the kind of person who will know what to do about a lying toaster.

"Why is your toaster lying?" he asks.

"It is jealous of me."

"That makes sense. Your toaster lives in a lower realm of being. It's only fair for it to be jealous of you."

"What should I do?" I ask.

"I had a similar problem with a bicycle once. It was terribly angry at me. It constantly devised plans to do away with me."

"What did you do?"

"I chopped it up into tiny pieces, pieces so small that the bike could no longer believe it was a bike. A bike with no identity has a hard time planning to kill you."

"Will I have to do that to my toaster?"

"I don't think so, your situation is less serious."

We take the toaster apart. The toaster can't do anything. The toaster can't lie when it's reduced to its components.

FICTION

One of its components is a computer.

"Why does the toaster have a computer?" I ask.

"I don't know. There shouldn't be a computer inside of the toaster. A toaster doesn't need a computer."

Computers aren't for toasters. Computers are for predicting the trends of the stock market or reading emails, not for the insides of toasters. The computer is why the toaster is lying.

We drive to the supermarket. Inside, we buy a large bottle of drain cleaner. We also buy two oranges. We drive back. We fill a glass bowl with drain cleaner and put the computer inside. It dissolves in a few hours. There is no difference between the computer and the drain cleaner anymore.

"That should solve the problem," he says.

"Yes."

We put the toaster back together without the computer that is now only a small part of the drain cleaner living inside a glass bowl. I turn the toaster on. I select the button marked "Five." It does not work. The toaster does nothing at all.

"The toaster is broken," I say.

"But it isn't lying."

"No, it isn't lying."

It is a nice day outside. The clouds drift lazily by, whispering prayers and condolences for the death of my lying toaster.

ROBIN GOW

A BRIEF SELF-HISTORY

screen saved into orange.
whirl & firework daddy perched
on the roof. a string
to tie all my worries up with.
do you know how to
wrap a present? i do not.
i wrap god in paper towels.
he's leaking milk all over
bathroom floors. windowsill all over
are giving up. a single bone
can vibrate into a new animal
or become a remote control.
tap water love-making. salt water cleanse.
keep a tray of salt
by the backdoor. i want to be
banished from somewhere.
handfuls of cherry tomatoes.
a coach to sleep on. spilling
from the ceiling fan. octopus me
in the bathtub tonight. i'm choking
on trumpet. i'm surrounded
by shrapnel. we talk
in hushed voices about
our last nickels. laundromats
open in my imagination. you cannot
love everyone just because
you love them. a chicken coop
for you & a chicken coop for me.
cracked wood. cracked
fingernails. a worried fissure

in the drywall. from the bathroom hole
i listen to my neighbor
cough & cough & cough. he's spitting
warships into the bathtub.
my soap melts quickly.
spider parachutes. my glass
forget-me-nots open like august.
whose pulse is this
behind the curtain? the last time i cried
all my tears turned to fat hot flies
so no thank you not
in this body. a backyard
on a CD. no entrance. not here.
there is a rough iron gate.
he loves me so much. he loves me
so very very much.

ROBIN GOW

GULPING

more than i can manage.
ears as acolyte bells. i ring
tuesday's doorbell & wait for the sun.
arriving is a series of stoops.
concrete hardens into the cast
of a poet's face. my uncle plays pacman
in the corner of a dead pizzaria.
he is full of quarters.
i peel back my skin
to find a swarm of beetles. shiny back.
all gems are just insects
with their legs pluck off
by miners. a shaft is waiting
in the basement.
i take a fork & a spoon
& whittle away at the earth.
dirt tastes like autumn. the seasons
have given up on me. it is just
summer summer summer. a tulip
where the light bulb should be.
the sound of losing the video game.
my uncle with his huge coarse hands
& a joystick toggling. i have
seven knees & five eyes.
a blinking ache
in my joints. who is going to change
the last light bulb? who is going
to unhinge sigh from his teeth.
i want a new finger to press
to the roof of the animal's mouth.

my vocabulary isn't strong enough
to tell you how the basement hurts.
remove the tooth & burry it.
we need more trees. how long will it take
for the seed to sprout. red leaves.
vein stem. the earth's core
is full of blood; hot & stewing.
somewhere the tea leaves are read
& suggest death. a tarot card is pulled
that means no one
is going to sleep tonight
i try to swallow a pencil but it gets stuck
& not a ghost writes poems
in my throat. who will become
a planet? who will unknot the necks
of trees from one another?
a bird is taking up oil paints.
i am the bird & there is no canvas
just a blank wall in my house
that has been staring at me.
i need to cover it's sixteen eyes.
maybe we were all angels
& then we were banished. i once
touched a boy's back & felt
where his wings used to be.
i once swallowed a boy & the next day
spat a tangle of ivy out
into the backyard. it is still
working its way up the mountain.
the planets roll down hill
& nestle with each other.
i turn a light out & cradle
my extra three eyes in the dark
before placing each in my mouth
one by one.

GRETA HAYER

THE WIVES OF ARTUR ELLIS

It used to be that in the village of Arbor, women were not born but plucked like fruit from the Great Tree to ripen into wives. On the last day of the harvest season, the villagers strung ribbons and bells from tall ladders. At noon, the young men of Arbor climbed the chiming ladders and picked a she-fruit from The Tree. Each man, when he reached a certain age, was permitted one fruit, instructed by the elders on how to tend to it, then spent the following days and weeks praying for a wife to burst from the fruit and be his.

Occasionally, the fruit did not turn into a wife; it grew tight and brown and hard. For the man who plucked it, his fate was sealed. He would have no wife for as long as he lived; he would grow old and die alone. Artur Ellis feared he was one of these men. As autumn deepened into winter and then lifted into spring, his she-fruit had shriveled from the size of a melon to that of a fist, a thin film of white mold growing along its wrinkled skin. While his age-mates trotted through the village with comely, soft-spoken wives, Artur was alone.

Artur pleaded with the elders but they would not let him choose a new fruit. "Yours still might grow into a wife," they said, but Artur had never seen a she-fruit take more than a few weeks to ripen, certainly not one that looked as dead as his.

Artur wondered what had done wrong. He kept it comfortable and warm and sang it lullabies when the night was darkest. He begged the fruit to grow, to become healthy, to ripen into a tender and beautiful woman who would bear him sons who would, in turn, pluck their own wives from The Tree. He whispered sweet nothings to the dried-up fruit, every gentle word he had ever heard, coaxing it like he would a wild animal. He did not understand why some wives blossomed while his died. Was it something he did? Had he merely picked a bad fruit and ill luck had sealed his fate?

It wasn't fair, Artur decided. He wanted a wife more than many of the men who had one. He *deserved* a wife. So on a warm night in early spring, Artur snuck from his cottage and crept down the road to the Great Tree and, by the light of the milky moon, snatched a she-fruit from the lowest branch. It wasn't harvest season, but The Tree was already filled with she-fruits. The one Artur picked was heavy as a pitcher of water, so large he had to carry it with both hands. He held it to his chest, the shadowy arms of the Great Tree stretching above him in every direction. The twigs curled like gnarled fingers snatching at the she-fruit throbbing against his skin, like it already had a heartbeat, as he hurried away.

After a few weeks, the new fruit was bigger than his old fruit, which he hid in a cupboard so no one suspected his theft. The stolen fruit grew quickly, its skin turning from pale green to a rich, vivid orange. It smelled of honeysuckle and Artur's mouth watered. He thrilled at the tales his age-mates told of their wedding nights, when the soft, golden-haired wives came eagerly to their new husbands to be tasted, their supple, rounded arms holding them tight.

At last, when his stolen she-fruit was the size of a bale of hay, Artur took his best bone knife and sliced into the thick skin. The flesh of the fruit split easily, white and pliant, and the scent of summer filled the cottage. He peeled long stretches of rind from the she-fruit, until finally, ambered and sticky as a fly in sap, his wife was before him, curled into a ball, long dark hair plastered to her skin. She was naked, freshly born.

Slowly, she lifted her head. Her eyes opened, the green of new leaves. "Who are you?" she asked.

"I'm your husband," Artur replied.

"No, you're not." She unfolded her body from its position. She was long-legged, thin and sharp of face, both thinner and sharper than Artur preferred in women, if he was honest.

"I plucked you from the Great Tree," he said, trying to stay calm.

He didn't want to argue with his new wife, not so soon after she emerged from the fruit.

The young woman shook her head. "No. I'm out of season." She tried to stand, but toppled, weak and uncoordinated as a fawn. Her sticky skin collected the dirt from the floor, muddying her arm. She tried to brush herself clean, but her hand came away dirty as well.

Artur lifted her in his arms, hesitant of the syrupy juice on her skin. He laid her on his bed, on the finest quilt he owned, and raised her hand to his lips. She tasted of lemons and peaches, sour and sweet at once. Her hand trembled as he licked the juice from each of her fingers. His tongue explored her knuckles, her palm, luxurious and slow. She tried to pull away, but he held fast.

"Don't do this," she said.

But Artur sucked the sweetness from her skin, licking the soft flesh of her pale wrist, the inside of her elbow. Each inch of her tasted slightly different. The valley between her breasts was floral, but behind her knee, she tasted more like an orange. She clenched her legs together, and he had to work them open with both hands. He felt a twist somewhere in his guts, a seedling of doubt. This wasn't in the stories the other men told. No one had spoken of an unwilling wife. He smothered the sensation in his stomach; this was how it was always done. It was a husband's duty to savor his bride, and he did so, though she cried salty tears as he cleaned her with his wet mouth.

Her name was Merwyn, and she was not a good wife. She didn't cook or clean, and she spent her days gazing out the slits in the shutters. Why couldn't she be like the other wives, who walked hand-in-hand with their husbands, negotiating prices for wheat and cooking warm suppers?

"Why are you like this?" Artur shouted one night, having come home to find every dish he owned dirtied and stacked on the table, the bed an unmade crumple of quilts. "You are the worst wife in all of Arbor."

"And you," she said with such venom that spit sprayed from her mouth, "you are the worst husband to ever pluck a woman from The Tree. No man should ever be allowed to pick a wife again."

Artur deflated and sank to his knees. "I didn't want to spend my life alone," he said, and his throat seized as though he was about to cry.

His wife examined him like a wad of dung on her boot. "You should not have done what you did. You should not have plucked me early."

Artur nodded in agreement. He had broken the one rule of the Great Tree. Of course, his stolen bride would harbor resentment. "I'm so sorry." He clutched at her skirts, and Merwyn stepped to the side, so only the filthy hem slipped through his fingers. "When my first fruit didn't ripen, I didn't think there was another way."

"You had another wife before me?"

"I had a fruit. It didn't become a wife."

"Show me." Her tone softened slightly. She seemed curious.

Artur went to the kitchen and pulled the wrinkled she-fruit from the cabinet. It looked even worse than before, like a dried fig, brown and small. It smelled faintly of rot.

"Give her to me," Merwyn said. "Please." Her voice tipped like she was asking a question. She sounded like a real wife.

Artur handed her the fruit. For the first time, Merwyn smiled.

After that night, Merwyn began to change. She accompanied him out into the village, let him lead her by the arm. She barely flinched at his touch. The other men in the village praised her beauty and Artur's luck. She was so much darker than the other wives—all of golden hair and soft with curves. Artur suspected that her coloring came from being plucked out of harvest, but no one seemed suspicious. The men of the village were simply happy for him. "I never thought your she-fruit would ripen," a friend confessed. "Thank the gods I was wrong."

But the oddest change in Merwyn was her fascination with the old she-fruit, the first one Artur had picked. She sat with it in her lap, slept with it pressed between her breasts. She petted the skin of it, spoke to it as she went about her chores. She told it secrets that she did not allow Artur to overhear.

And the old she-fruit began to respond in a way it had never done for Artur. The fuzz of mold retreated; the skin regained a healthy shine. It swelled swiftly. One day, coming home from the fields, Artur found the rind of she-fruit curled and empty on the dirt floor and Merwyn cleaning a yellow-haired girl with a sponge and a bucket of water.

"Her name is Agnesse," Merwyn informed him, and the two wives slept in his bed that night, leaving no room for him.

No man was supposed to have two wives. It was why men were allowed only one she-fruit, whether it ripened or not, to prevent the exact situation in which Artur Ellis found himself. Agnesse would simply have to stay in the cottage, hidden, until he could concoct a solution.

"What happens if the elders find out about her?" Merwyn asked.

Artur hesitated. Most likely, he would be banished from Arbor, but he had no idea what would happen to the wives themselves. They couldn't be reassigned to other husbands, and they couldn't remain unwed.

"You'll be sent away," he lied.

Agnesse held fast to Merwyn's hand. "No!" she exclaimed, genuinely horrified. Agnesse seemed sweet and kind, the opposite of Merwyn's tartness. The right kind of wife. He felt the tickle of a fantasy. Perhaps someone would find out, and maybe *Merwyn* would be banished, and he could live the rest of his life here with Agnesse. But no, he told himself, that kind of scenario didn't seem likely at all.

Deeply set in anxiety, Artur drank at the tavern until late in the evening.

"You don't want a wife, do you?" he asked his age mate Tristen, whose she-fruit hadn't ripened.

"Are you offering yours?" Tristen laughed and tipped the rest of his ale into his wide mouth. The tavern was mostly empty, with only a few young men who didn't yet have wives and a few older men who had grown tired of theirs.

"No," Artur said, dejected. Of course, he couldn't just give away one of his wives. Someone was bound to find out. "But your fruit hasn't grown."

Tristen shrugged. "Never really wanted a wife."

Artur found it hard to believe. Why would a man not want a wife? When he arrived home to see his Merwyn and Agnesse, curled together in bed, nothing but skin separating their hearts, it seemed that even his wife had found a wife. He lay upon the rug and felt even lonelier than he had before.

Agnesse's hair stretched from her crown to the tips of her fingers, and Merwyn brushed it with an ivory comb. The two wives whispered together, Agnesse's soft, round face close to Merwyn's strong, angular one. They were so different. Artur had the suspicion that, if Merwyn hadn't been there to corrupt her, Agnesse would have been the perfect wife.

"Your hair is so beautiful," Artur said, reaching out to stroke it. It was softer than velvet.

"Please don't touch me." She stepped behind Merwyn, who glared at him in a way he had never thought wives could glare.

Artur left the cabin, though it was not a day he had to work the fields. He went to the tavern until dark.

The next day, Agnesse's hair was shorn as short as a man's. Few of the other wives ever cut their hair and certainly not without permission from their husbands. Artur felt like she had somehow disobeyed him. He watched the happy, docile wives of the other villagers, wishing his were more like them.

Many drinks later, Artur stumbled down the cobbled road. In the center of town was the Great Tree, thick as a wagon wheel and tall as the clouds. The Tree blocked the stars with its twisting branches and heavy green she-fruits hung just out of reach.

"Curse you!" he shouted at The Tree, the drink fumbling his tongue. "Curse your damnable harvest."

The Tree stood, adamant. In the knots and swirls of bark, it seemed as though eyes gazed out, blank and unashamed.

Artur kicked at a root, but it did not budge. His biggest toe throbbed, and he hobbled home. Again, he slept on the rug at the foot of the bed.

The morning was overbright and loud. The sounds of his wives felt as raucous as the town market. He held the blanket over his eyes, the only blanket not commandeered by Merwyn and Agnesse. "What in the names of the gods," he said, rising from the rug.

Merwyn looked over at him. She stood in the doorway, talking to the butcher's wife. "Good, you're awake."

Artur looked around. His cabin was filled with baskets, buckets, and a wheelbarrow. There was hardly space to move about. Agnesse stood in the kitchen, stacking a set of wide wooden bowls. The butcher's wife handed Merwyn a metal tub and whispered something in her ear. She left swiftly. "What's going on?" He tried not to shout but he was in a sour mood. "She saw Agnesse!"

Merwyn looked as though she was about to shout back, but Agnesse laid a hand on her forearm. "It's all right, dear husband," Agnesse said. "We'll have everything out of here tomorrow."

Agnesse was such a good wife, thought Artur. "But the butcher's wife saw you."

"She won't tell the elders." Agnesse smiled at him.

"Please be more careful. I don't want anything to happen to you." He said this looking pointedly at Agnesse, not Merwyn.

"I'll take care of her, don't worry." Merwyn placed a smack of a kiss on Agnesse's cheek.

Who was she to protect Agnesse? She was just a wife. "You wouldn't be here if it weren't for me," he said.

"I don't want to be here," she said.

Artur left in a huff.

Merwyn and Agnesse did not wake Artur the next day, but the village's uproar did. He shuffled to his window and opened the shutters a crack, careful not to let in light and wake his sleeping wives. Their arms tangled around each other in his bed, their connection evident even in the dark.

Many people had gathered in the street, heading toward the center of town. "Have you seen?" The miller asked the blacksmith loud enough for Artur to overhear. "The Great Tree?"

The miller hurried down the street, the blacksmith not far behind. Artur could see a crowd moving in the direction of The Tree. He fumbled with his dressing robe in the dark and slipped out the door, bare feet cold on the cobblestones.

The people were gathered at the base of the Great Tree, just like at the plucking festival, except, instead of laughter and joyous exclamations, the men were shouting, angry, and shaking their fists.

The women leaned into each other, eyes wide.

Above them, the arching, massive branches of the Great Tree, green with leaves and moss, was barren. Not even the smallest she-fruit hid in the foliage.

"How will we get wives now?" a man cried out.

The women exchanged glances and secrets, their hands shielding their words. The men exchanged threats.

"Whoever did this—"

"When I catch the culprit—"

Eventually, the crowd dispersed, loud and confused. Artur stood until the last villager had left. He had a bad feeling in his gut. Merwyn. If it hadn't been for her, everything would have stayed the same. There would be a wife to harvest for every man. He cursed her under his breath, then returned to his cottage, feet bloody and sore.

In his home, Artur did not have two wives waiting for him, but seven, no, eight. They congested his small cottage, some partially dressed and most of them still sticky. Their rinds lay on the floor, filling the space with the pungent scent of citrus, nearly overpowering. They were dark as Merwyn, not a golden head among them. They chattered like a flock of crows, but they stopped speaking as he entered. Now that the day's light filled the cottage, he could see more fruit of various sizes, stacked on every surface, piled in the corners. They filled the baskets, the wheelbarrow, even a small cart. The fruit were in various stages of ripeness, some hard and green like limes, others plumper than pumpkins.

"It was you!" Artur shouted at Merwyn. "You picked all the she-fruit."

"What if it was?" Merwyn stood tall against him, nose to nose. "Why should anyone be able to pick a wife from The Tree? Why should any woman be forced to become a wife?"

"That is the way things are done," he shouted. The silence and the scent of the room deepened to a nauseating sweetness. A headache twinged at his temples.

Merwyn, her green eyes narrowed, growled. A feral look crossed her face and for a moment he felt fear, fear of a wife, which was ludicrous. His fear turned to anger, the kind of hot fury that seeps as tears from one's eyes, wet and flushed. "You are the worst wife. I wish I could be rid of you," he said.

Merwyn smiled, not in mirth but in triumph. "Good. Then I'll no longer bother you. I am no longer your wife."

A murmur spread through the wives in the cottage, excited, even delighted. Another woman burst from a fruit, naked. She unfolded her long limbs and stood behind Agnesse. She seemed to understand precisely what was going on, perhaps more so than Artur himself.

"We're leaving," Merwyn said. "Come, my sweets. We're off."

A wife clapped, others giggled. They tore the sheets from Artur's bed and wrapped themselves. Some dressed in Artur's own clothes; others knotted the fine quilt over their sticky breasts. They hoisted fruit-filled bushels to their hips and carried trays balanced high with she-fruit. Merwyn led them out the door, sparing but a glance at Artur, her eyes a blade.

Agnesse passed, and she smelled like spring itself. Then she slipped outside, joining the beautiful, laughing parade.

Other women from the village spied the wives of Artur Ellis as they walked out of town. Some grabbed shawls and baskets of bread and joined them, bidding their husbands goodbye with a wave or a blown kiss. Some stayed by the side of those men who had plucked them, but many women drifted into the streets, then away with the crowd.

Artur watched them leave until the wives turned a corner on the path away from town. He returned to his cottage. It was empty of fruit and women. It suddenly seemed very large and very lonely. It was only then that he realized what he had done, why Merwyn hated him, and no wife could love him. He had made so many mistakes. He put his head in his hands and wept.

The Great Tree remained barren and never grew another she-fruit. Over-plucked, the elders said, but Artur knew it was his fault for what he had done to Merwyn. The seasons passed without more wives, and though husbands died, Artur Ellis never found another woman who would agree to be his.

And that is why, in the village of Arbor, women are no longer plucked from the Great Tree. Without wives, the town withered and died, but stories are often told of the women who walked away, who settled in other villages and spread through the land. They are said to be the boldest and bravest of all women, dark of hair and sharp of tongue, but if one ever loves you, they say you can taste sweetness in her mouth and smell the scent of citrus long after she has left the room.

CHARTS, 2NDARY & 3RTIARY

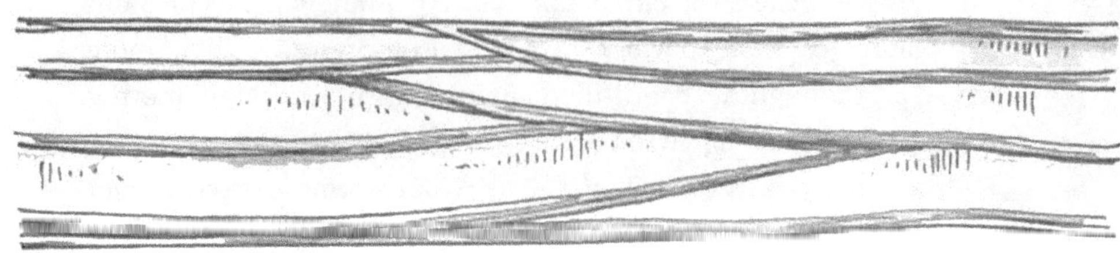

Extrapolation of Methantrambulated Intravenous Protuberance Coalescence Over Preceding N^th^ Æons, indicating patterns of intersection indicating preferential tendencies indicating contraindications sublimating supraindications with regard to any indicatory elements

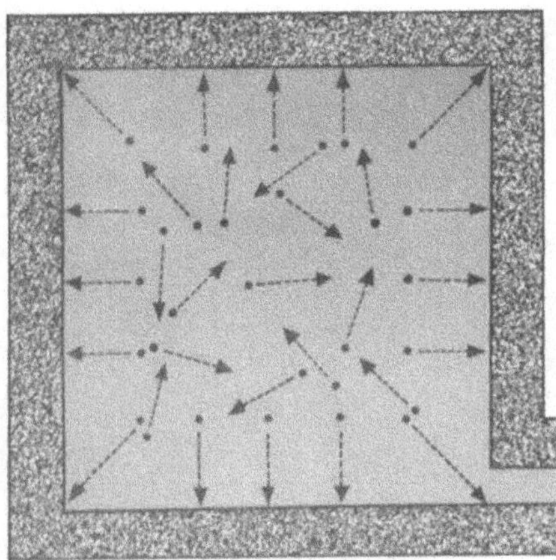

Coördinated Dance Moves During Intercosmic Singles, Doubles, and N-tuples Mixer, so you can practice your moves because no one likes a Fumbling Fragnorg

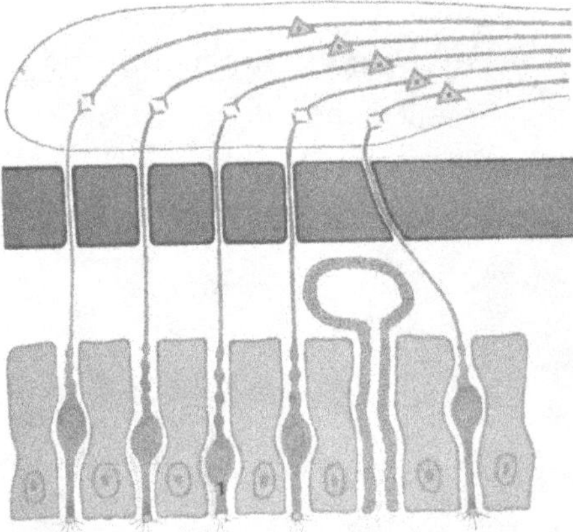

Charting Panpsychic Combobulations Through Permeable Realities in the Twenty-Second and Twenty-Seventh Strings, shown here w/o multiplicities of perception

Fully-Articulated & -Reticulated Depiction of Greg's Deontological Non-Hierarchical Inarticulability Article w/ Cardinal Anarchical Obstacles & Accidental Particle Particularity & Peculiarity Arsenals feat. Critically Unstoppable Non-Remarkable Verticals

Frog, Not Dead

REBECCA HIGGINS

TELL ME

"STANDING IN FRONT OF A TRAIN to kill yourself is selfish," my dad tells me. His friend, a train conductor, was going sixty miles per hour when he saw someone standing on the tracks. Pulling the brakes, the wheel screeched beneath him. It would take a mile to stop. Too far. "All you can do is lay on the horn and close your eyes."

"When you were a baby, you'd cry louder if I held you," my dad tells me. Later, my mom tells me that he had to wait until I was asleep to hold me.

"If someone is attacking you and you get them on the ground, stomp on their neck and run away," my dad tells me. "They aren't going to get up, but you don't want to hear the sounds they'll make after you crush their windpipe."

"Be more careful," my dad tells me. He saw the parallel lines on my arm. I tell him about a board with staples cutting me. I lied.

"Mass shooters that shoot themselves afterward should've just shot themselves," my dad tells me. "Save the ammunition."

"Give me your arm," my dad tells me. I pull up my sleeve and reach my arm out. He cradles my arm, looking at the cuts. He holds me and cries.

"If someone is ever bothering you at a store, yell, 'Dad,'" my dad tells me. "Even if I'm not there, another dad will come and help you."

"You can see the union's therapist for free," my dad tells me. "I can take you."

"Get whatever you want," my dad tells me. I smile and fill up the cart at Trader Joe's. "As long as you eat it."

"Here is my work email," my dad tells me. "If there's something you don't want to tell me in person, you can say it there. I won't tell anyone."

"You don't have to be nice," my dad tells me. "If someone is bothering you, you can stand up for yourself.

"I will drive you to the therapy appointment," my dad tells me. "But we have to go an hour early to drop off aluminum. Then I don't have to lie to your mother and sister about where we were."

"You might as well live under a bridge," my dad tells me. I just told him about my plan to study creative writing. "Save your money."

"I can be here in eight hours if you need me," my dad tells me. We used command hooks to hang Christmas lights and now it's time for him to leave me at college. "I just need an hour to tell work that I won't be there and get a bag at home. If you don't want mom to know, I'll just tell her I'll be out of town for a couple days and that I'm not cheating on her."

"If someone's following you, go to a house with toys in the yard," my dad tells me. "That means they have kids. You should be safe there."

"Your mother told me that you are taking antidepressants," my dad tells me. "She needed to tell someone. Don't be mad at her."

"Killing yourself isn't an option," my dad tells me. Two of his coworkers' kids committed suicide within a month of each other. He looks at me with drying tears. "You know that, right?"

"There are more side effects to your medication than just dry mouth," my dad tells me. He says three weeks after the Parkland shooting. After he discovered that the shooter also took Zoloft.

"How are you doing?" my dad asks whenever it is just the two of us.

"I am still going," I tell him. "Like a train."

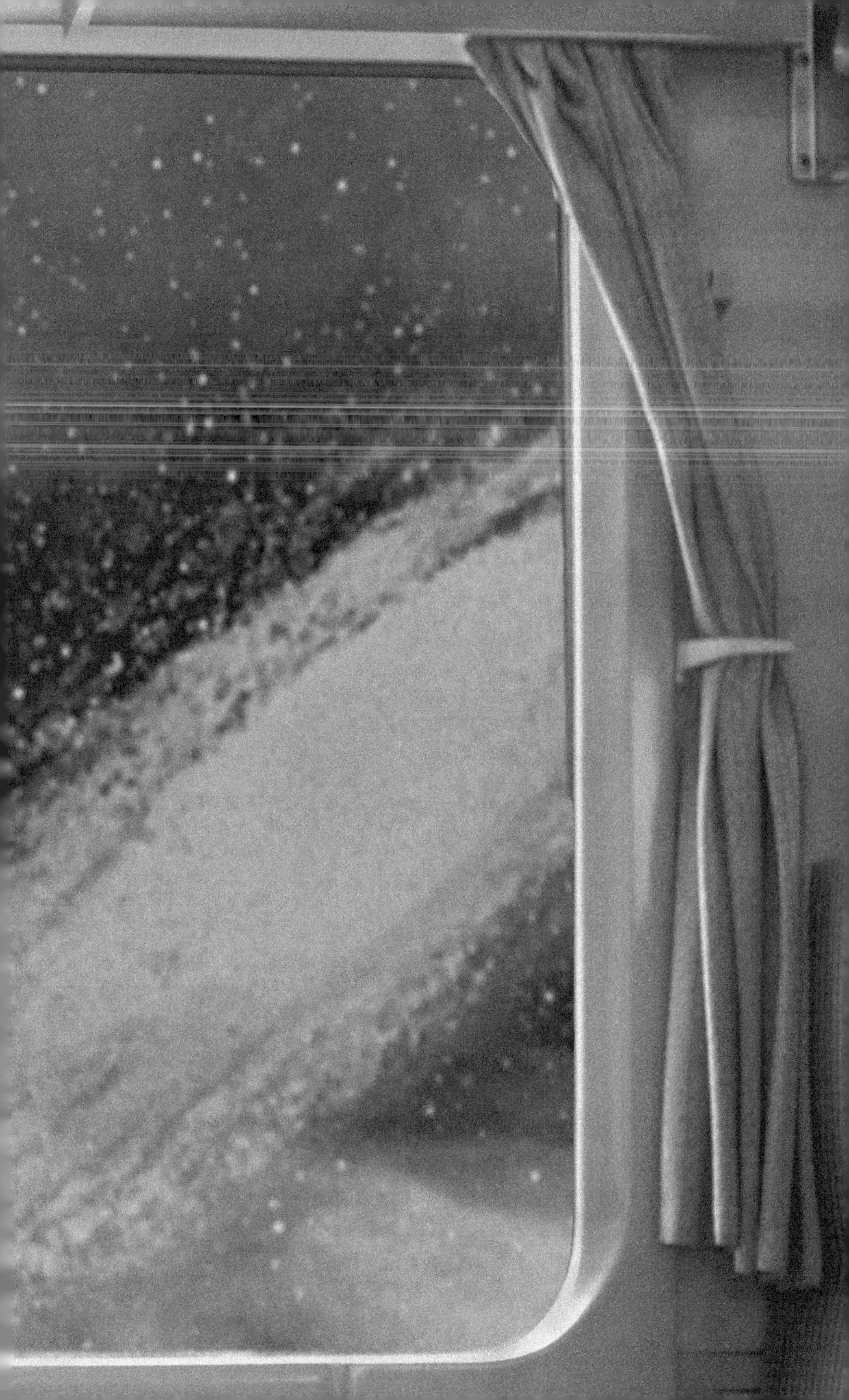

GIFT SHOP

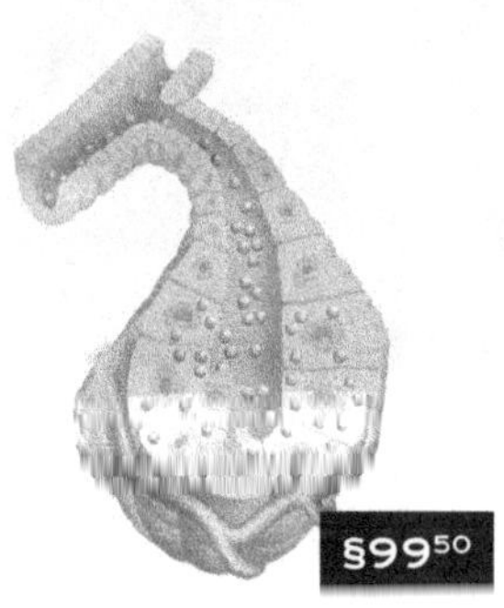

TREMBLAY'S INSOLE

A fantastic way to pamper your tired old feet, hooves, tentacles, or any other appendage terminus in true interdimensional style.

HEART OF BROCOL'II

This pulsating stone from the core of the long dead planet Brocol'ii will recalibrate your Circadian polyrhythms.

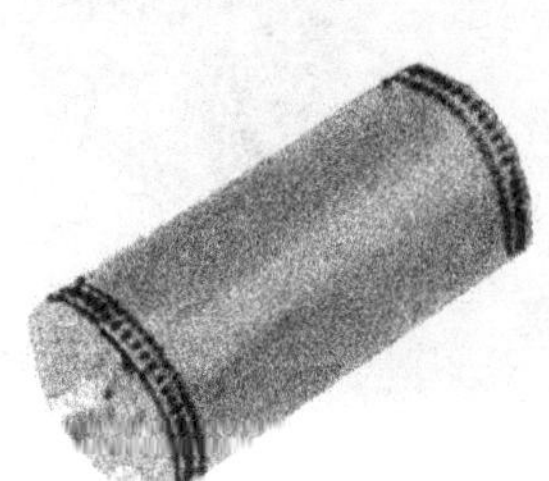

PRO-DUX PREMIUM

Whatever your challenge, this premium product will keep you covered. Rest assured that you have the only product for your project, every time.

MISGEOMETRIC MANIFESTATION

A physical remnant of the Great Geometry Wars of Interspemulon XIX, these artifacts can exist only in a void of unmathematics (not included).

OBLIV-I-BUDDY

The only doll designed to comfort both children and adults as they reckon with the fact that we're all hurtling toward an infinite void!

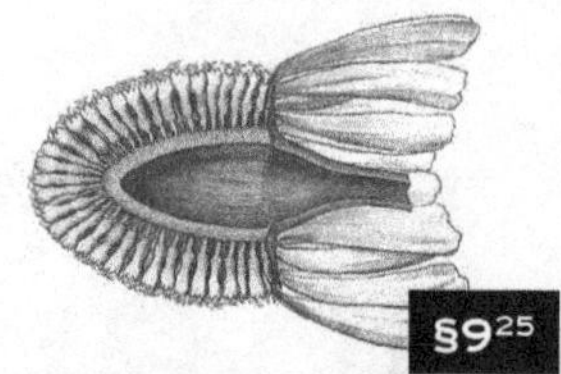

WADSWORTH'S FABULOUS FLYING DENTATUS

Invented by the inestimable Dr. Perfidious X. X. L. Wadsworth, these toothsome flappers can bite any hard-to-reach items.

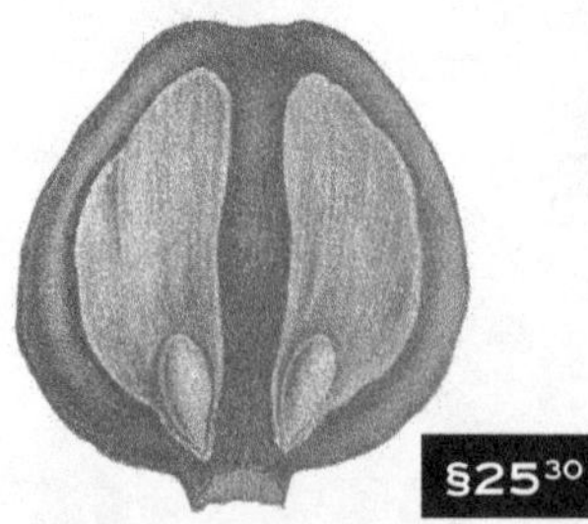

NEWTON'S FIG

Feeling too light? This little miracle drastically increases the effects of gravity.

GRUNTHOR LEAVINGS

The best product on the market to liberate you from the shackles of linear chronology. It's time to make time your own.

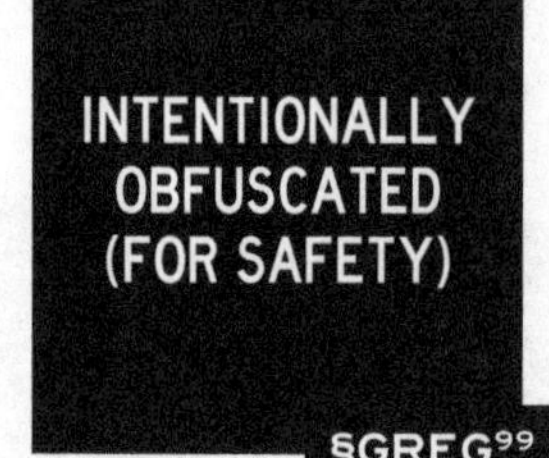

GREG (NOT PICTURED)

Do you need an extra Greg (madness-inducing if reduced to 2-D)? Get one delivered right to your seat!

CASEY McCONAHAY

I'D JUST AS SOON KISS A WOOKIE

THEY MET AT A *STAR WARS* CONVENTION in Youngstown, Ohio. He'd come as Bib Fortuna, the Twi'lek majordomo of the space gangster Jabba the Hutt. She was Maz Kanata, the proprietor of an interstellar tavern on the planet Takodana. When they saw one another across the carpeted ballroom of a busy Ramada Inn, they were drawn together as though he was the *Millennium Falcon* and she was the tractor beam of the original Death Star.

He sat beside her at a panel discussion featuring voice actors from the animated Clone Wars series. She touched his Twi'lek lekku and told him that what she found most attractive about his costume was that he'd not chosen a predictable character—not Darth Maul or Boba Fett or any member of the Jedi Order—but someone obscure enough that only the most dedicated *Star Wars* fans would know him.

"We have that in common," she told him. "Our dedication."

He could scarcely see her eyes behind her thick, tinted goggles.

"I've watched *The Empire Strikes Back* three hundred and seventy-one times," he told her.

"The theatrical release or the 1997 special edition?"

"The theatrical release three hundred and sixty-five times. The special edition six."

They spent the day together. They learned that he lived in Warren, Ohio, and she lived in Niles.

"That's under twelve parsecs away," he told her.

Then they laughed as though they'd never heard anything funnier.

They met again a week later. She was Boushh, Leia's bounty hunter alter-ego. He was the smuggler Nien Nunb. Their server at the Applebee's looked at them as though they were visitors from another planet.

"But we are from another planet," she said. "I'm from Alderaan, and you're from Sullustan."

"And this is like the Mos Eisley Cantina but without the music."

"Or Ponda Baba."

"Or Greedo."

"Or Han."

Midway through a conversation about whether Han shot first—they both agreed that he had—she told him that it was good that they met in costume.

"Because it's not about looks," she said. "Because we love each other for who we really are."

Later that evening, they played *Battlefront II* on the PlayStation in his apartment. She took off her helmet. They kissed. She put the helmet back on.

"We should stay," she said, "in costume."

They slept in makeup and masks. Not in clothes.

"A marathon?" she asked him.

"A marathon."

She wore the white garments of Taun We, aide to the prime minister of Kamino. He made popcorn in the kitchen, and she watched from the doorway.

"In what order?" she asked him. "By *Star Wars* universe chronology or by date of original theatrical release?"

Popcorn pinged in the microwave.

"You decide," he told her.

She held the replica lightsaber that he'd purchased at a Galaxy's

Edge attraction at Disneyland. Examining it for authenticity, she told him, "Let's watch the prequel trilogy tonight and the original trilogy next weekend. So we'll have something to look forward to."

He wore his best Jedi robes. She watched the films in his arms.

"How many times have you seen *Attack of the Clones*?" she asked him.

"One hundred forty-two times. And you?"

"Two hundred nineteen. Don't judge me. It's a beautiful love story."

The one hundred and forty-third time he watched *Attack of the Clones* was by far the most memorable. It was the first time he watched it with her.

It was a work function, she told him. A formal event. She led him to her closet and asked him, "What should I wear?"

He said, "You have more costumes than Padme Amidala, Queen of the Naboo."

She showed him her Padme Amidala costumes. He chose the black dress worn by Padme's decoy in *The Phantom Menace.*

"Perfect," she told him.

It was an ornate dress. It took her hours to get ready. He'd rented a tuxedo and changed clothes in her living room, and as he waited for her to finish, he watched some episodes of *Star Wars Resistance.*

She was upset when she saw him.

"Where is your costume?" she asked.

"My costume?"

"You aren't dressed like a *Star Wars* character."

"You said it was a formal event."

"You could have come as Senator Bail Organa. You could have dressed like Luke Skywalker in the medal ceremony at the end of

Star Wars: A New Hope."

"Or Palpatine when he was Supreme Chancellor."

"Or Palpatine when he was Supreme Chancellor. Exactly."

He straightened his black rented bowtie.

"I don't have any of those costumes," he said. "I don't have that many costumes."

"Let's not go."

"But you said—"

"I'll look stupid. Dressed like this. Christ. You're wearing a tux."

When they met the next evening, she was no longer angry.

"I should have told you," she said. "I could have bought you some clothes. I forgive you. It wasn't your fault."

She wore the loose garments of Mon Mothma, a leader of the Galactic Senate. He was Cassian Andor.

"When I get married," she told him, "I'm wearing Padme Amidala's wedding dress. And my groom will wear Anakin Skywalker's formal robes."

He touched the charm of her Mon Mothma necklace.

"What if your groom doesn't want to?"

"Dear, he won't have a choice. If we marry, he'll wear what I say."

They went to laser tag once in their costumes. She was Enfys Nest, the leader of the Cloud Riders. He was an armored Knight of Ren.

"Take a look around," he told her when they were surrounded by a swarm of foul-mouthed teenagers. "You know what's about to happen. You know what we're up against."

She held her laser-gun close. He heard her breaths through her mask.

"We need you," she told him.

"What about what you need?"

A beam of light shot above them.

"I don't know what you're talking about," she said.

"You probably don't."

"And what precisely am I supposed to know?"

He crouched with her beneath a wide wooden obstacle. He looked out from behind it. There were more teenagers than he could count.

"Attacking those teenagers isn't my idea of courage," he said. "It's more like suicide."

She turned away from him.

"Well," she told him. "Take care of yourself then. I guess that's what you're best at, isn't it?"

They died in an assault of laser-gun flashes.

"Sorry," he told her, but she didn't say anything.

"Sorry," he said again.

Driving home from the laser tag arena, "Is something wrong?" he asked.

She didn't answer. Her face was concealed by her mask, and if something was wrong, it was impossible to tell.

She was dressed as an Imperial stormtrooper. He was C-3PO, the golden translator droid, and when she asked him to tell her something in Jawa, he shrugged his shoulders and told her that he couldn't speak any of the *Star Wars* languages.

"Not even Wookie?" she asked him.

"Not even Wookie."

They sat together in her living room. He asked her to tell him all the things that he didn't know about her—where she was from originally, whether she had siblings, what music she listened to—but she wouldn't answer him.

"None of that matters," she told him. "Let's just talk about *Star Wars*."

He took the mask from his head and put the mask by his side. He touched the white plastic helmet that she wouldn't remove.

"I loved you," he told her.

"I know."

He put the mask on his head again and went from the couch. Leaving her apartment for the last time, he told her, "I am not the droid you're looking for."

"No," she answered. "You are not the droid I'm looking for."

MARY LYNN REED

DOWNTOWN

THE BOYS ARE STONED AGAIN and that means pizza. We go to the tiny place on 68th. An Armenian soap opera is playing on the TV suspended above the counter. The sound is full of static and the acting is bad. Pepperoni for Kenny. Cheese, cheese, extra, extra, says Peter. I sliver myself around the front table. Thin, light, barely there, I tuck myself into the windowsill, sit with knees pretzeled. I lay my head against the cool concrete wall, feel its depressions against my brow as I watch the stream of taxis pour down Columbus Avenue. It's dusk and headlights flip on, two by two, cabs trolling for fares heading downtown. After dark, the city is a river of lights, constantly flowing.

A homeless guy sits on the street corner across from the pizza place, next to the ATMs. He holds a cardboard sign that says, "Need money for beer." A woman pushes a double-wide stroller past him, shakes her head. Twins. A boy and a girl, side-by-side, tiny hands reaching for the other's. I want to press my forehead against each of the babies'; I want to hear their secret language. They would never let me in; Tag and I never let anyone in. A man in a pink tie tosses the homeless guy a dollar.

When my brother Tag and I moved to Manhattan three years ago, he took the lower quadrant, East Village, and I claimed the Upper West Side, spreading our inheritance across the island, a desperate salve that healed nothing. He lived in a loft on St. Mark's with great morning sun, where he painted and drank. He didn't need a job but he took one at a gallery, installing other people's art. I went to auditions; I never ate; I started screwing Kenny, and I stood up my therapist every other week.

Tag used to call me from his loft in the middle of the night. "Tell me what you hear out your window," he'd say.

FICTION

And I'd tell him about the birds. So many birds, singing—loud—at all hours of the day. Songbirds, chirping birds, squawking birds, illogically drowning out all the other city sounds. Then Tag would hold the phone up to his window, letting me hear the East Village.

Music, the clinking of glasses, laughter, street noise.

"It's relentless," he said. "I never sleep."

Pizza slices on paper plates slide across the table and the boys flop in plastic chairs. I pull my legs together. I'm still wearing my black nylons even though Kenny scraped the hell out of them that morning in the alley off 79th. "Can't wait," he said. "Can't."

Kenny is beautiful in the way only boys can be beautiful. Deep dark eyes and thick lashes. He was my brother Tag's best friend. He says being with me is almost consolation.

Kenny and Peter and I have lived this way for nine months now. We do the same things; we make each other crazy; and we never go lower than 59th. We got into a cab once, about two months ago, and I said, "St. Mark's" before I realized. Peter and I were paralyzed, but Kenny corrected our course, telling the driver, "Columbus Circle. Stop there."

Now Kenny eats his pizza backwards, crust first. He rolls the rest into a ball and nibbles it like a rabbit. Peter fills the air with that high, raucous laugh that means nothing.

In junior high, Peter was a track star, a middle-distance runner with a smooth, agile stride. He was in our class but younger by two years. Tag, the magnetic field of misfits, brought him into our orbit.

"He's a genius," Tag said. "Geniuses are fragile because they know too much. That makes them beautiful, too."

In high school, Peter carried a small notebook, scribbling ideas and stolen bits of dialogue. He could recite Shakespeare, the ancient Greeks, Tennessee Williams. His own plays were philosophical rants with wild emotional swings, perfect for highlighting an actor's sensitivity and depth. He produced Kenny's first showcase in the city. Mine, too.

Tag was in love with Peter from the start but he waited until Peter was seventeen to seduce him. I always thought of them as casual lovers. Not permanent or serious. But loss can magnify devotion and I respect that. Grieving Tag is not a contest. The three of us are not competitors. We exist in antagonistic symbiosis. We don't talk about it. We've never been able to form the words.

In the pizza place, I look through the boys the way they look through me. They never ask if I want to eat because I always say no. My stomach is a clenched fist, unyielding. There are two women sitting at the far back table. One is round-faced and wears a man's long-sleeve shirt, Oxford, button-down. Her hair is cut short, clean, part on the side, the way Tag used to wear his. The other woman is tall and slim. She wraps a black shawl around her shoulders. She moves like the famous. I don't recognize her but I think I should; I want to know what roles she's played, what stage she commands. She leans forward and says something I can't hear; the other tucks her head into her shoulder, and blushes. The tall one takes the other's fingers into her hands, kisses them slowly. I imagine them in a sun-filled apartment, making love all morning and into the afternoon. They both wear a glassy-eyed daze, as if that's exactly where they'd been. I imagine them under a pile of soft blankets, taking solace in the brush of smooth skin.

They are not young women. They have wrinkles and laugh lines and they are feeding each other pizza. The tall woman places her hand against her lover's face. They stare into each others' eyes. The shawl falls off the woman's shoulder. She turns her body slightly away, then reaches into her bag, pulls out a cell phone. Her expression clouds.

The sky is dark now, and the city lights flicker white, red, alive.

We missed the Improvisation Workshop again. None of us have had an audition in months. In the afternoon, we fell asleep on the rocks in the park until the ballfields crawled with kids after school, their shrill voices echoing off the jagged, cold stone. Peter woke up swearing: at the kids, the sun, at the dogs barking, at Kenny.

"Where's the shit? Give me the shit!"

Kenny's chin dug into my side and I felt a little sick, while Peter kept yelling. "Gimme the shit. Where's the shit?" Until Kenny pulled out the bag, handed it to him.

"Not here," Kenny said.

We stopped near the wall by the playground where the foliage is thick. I strained to hear a chorus of invisible birds while the two of them finished off our weed. My eyes closed, I tried to conjure Tag's voice, his smile. The memories are jagged and rough. I would force them if I could, rip them through muscle and bone.

Now Peter is shoving an entire slice of pizza into his mouth, folded over. Grease drips down his chin. His blond hair is clumped and dirty, his shirt is buttoned askew. I wonder how long it's been since he went home to his mother and three little sisters in Brooklyn who adore him. His family is alive and they love him and yet here he is, with us. I want to push him out the door, tell him to grow up. To move on. Before I can, Peter jumps out of his chair, yelling, "I'm wet. Wet. Everywhere wet!"

He pushes Kenny, sends him rocking against the table. "Did you spill something on me? Where did it come from?"

Kenny's in a daze. He's farther away than I am.

When we were kids, Kenny had a red bicycle with white rim tires. He rode it up and down the block, as slow as he could without stopping, steering with one finger. Tag and I watched from our front stoop as he rode back and forth. Entire lifetimes pass on front stoops in Brooklyn.

Tag leaned into me once, whispered, "James Dean's Schwinn."

Remembering this, I laugh out loud. Peter spins around. "Why do you always take his goddamned side?"

Peter hates me for reasons he doesn't understand. The instinct is buried deep in his animal brain. Yet there are times when he can't take his eyes off me. He searches for Tag in my face, without apology. I don't blame him. I do it sometimes, too. In the mirror.

On the TV above our heads, a woman with enormous breasts is weeping. Her chest heaves, and Kenny smirks.

Peter pulls a quarter out of his pocket, rubs it down his pant leg. "It's wet. Feel—"

He presses the coin against Kenny's arm. "Feel!" he says, grabbing Kenny's hand.

Kenny brushes him off. "Don't touch me, Fruit Loop. You're wasted. Eat more pizza."

The two women in the back are looking at us. The round-faced one catches my eye. She's boyish and plain, and I'm filled with a strange urgency to know her name. She's not intriguing in the way of her elegant lover. But I want to name them both.

Tag and Katrina. He called me Kat. No one else but Tag called me Kat.

"I'm leaking," Peter says. "I'm leaking out of my pores."

I press my forehead against the window. Its panes are double thick. I can see the women in my peripheral vision. The tall one stares at Kenny. Her brow is furrowed, as if she's puzzling out an equation. Kenny gets out of his chair, grips Peter's shoulders.

"You're dry as a bone," he says. "I wouldn't lie to you. O.K.?"

"You can't feel it? You really can't?" Peter says. I'm afraid he's going to cry. It happens sometimes.

The guys behind the pizza counter nudge each other. The Armenian soap opera goes to commercial. They mute the TV.

Kenny puts his arm around Peter. "Another slice?"

A cell phone rings, loud enough to turn everyone's head. One of those ear-piercing classic-phone ring tones, as if we're sitting in a 1970s trailer park in Arizona or Texas. That sound doesn't belong here. It's an aberration.

The tall woman clutches the ringing beast to her chest. Briskly, she heads toward our table, the door, the street, her face sliced with harsh angles. Her voice is deep and frazzled as she answers, "Meeting went long. Leaving work right now. Yes. Yes. I'm on my way."

She barely makes it out the door and then she's back, tucking the phone deep in the pocket of her snug jeans. She tilts her head up. Her lips are moving but she's not speaking. She's calculating something, counting 1, 2, 3 as she returns to the table where the lover is waiting.

Peter is still mumbling, "Wet, wet," as if he were the only unstable boy in the world.

Between a paper plate and a Coke can, four hands entwine on the women's table. No words. No more smiles. The tall one stands up again, wraps her shawl across her body, loops her bag over her shoulder. She walks their trash to the dispenser. The other slips in beside her, compliant. Her shape isn't as boyish as her haircut and face. Her shirt is tucked neatly into black trousers. Her curves are not hidden, hips not shy. The two women melt into one another, navigating the small space without letting go. Their movements are fluid and unrehearsed.

The pizza counter guys watch them. Kenny watches, too.

I want to stand but I stop halfway, sitting on the table like a centerpiece at Thanksgiving. I reach for Kenny, and Kenny holds onto Peter, and as the women brush past, holding hands, for a fraction of a second, we're a human chain, connected. Me, Kenny, Peter, the tall woman, and her lover. As they leave, the two women grapple to be closer. They would occupy the same skin if they could; I can feel it.

When they're gone, the fist in my stomach tightens. I watch them out the window as they walk to Columbus Avenue. They kiss, then the tall woman hails a cab, gets in alone. The other buries her hands in her pockets, and after the taxi pulls away, she doesn't move for a long time.

Taillights, people, billboards on buses. The woman left behind stands on the curb.

No one knows what my brother Tag meant to me. No one knows who we were to each other. Fraternal means less, they say. Two eggs and two sperm. Just siblings born on the same day. Biology tells us nothing about the soul. There is no explanation for desire.

Kenny was Tag's best friend. Peter was his lover for years. And neither of them had any idea. They still don't.

Peter sits down, takes a sip of his soda, and tells Kenny: "I want something. Call Javier."

The sound returns on the TV; the channel is switched to soccer.

Kenny pulls out his cell, begins thumbing out a text.

I look back out the window but the woman is no longer there.

Does she live in the city? Does she go back to an apartment, or a hotel. When will the lovers meet again? How deep do their secrets go? Does anyone know who they are to each other. I wonder how it will end.

Kenny smells of sweat and pepperoni. Into his ear, I whisper, "Downtown."

He stops typing, studies Peter's face for a long beat, then says, "He's not ready."

Peter finishes his soda, and chants: "Javier. Javier."

I wrap my arms around Kenny's neck, and he lifts me off the table. I am a feather. A fleck of dust. Confetti.

"Tonight," I whisper.

He pretends not to hear.

Outside, the air is stale with exhaust and garbage. An oily green residue lines the sidewalk. Kenny and I step around it; Peter walks right through.

Kenny's cell phone vibrates. His voice notches up an octave. "Javier's holding, up on 93rd."

"Yes," says Peter, "All right," and he's already walking.

"I'm going," I say. "Right now."

I stop where the two women parted. The traffic light changes and I raise my hand toward the taxis.

Kenny looks up the street toward Peter. "I can't leave him like this," he says. "He's wasted. And you're not."

"I never am." I try to meet his eyes but he won't let me. I wonder if he's ever seen me at all.

A taxi pulls up and I get in. "3rd Avenue and St. Mark's," I tell the driver, and don't look back.

The quick thrust of speed jostles me left and right. I press against the slick leather seat, trying to hold myself in place. I feel Tag there, in that moment. I look over, squinting to see his preppy boy haircut and wire rimmed glasses, but it's the blur of buildings, the fleeting familiarities sweeping past the window. The cab slows as Times Square fills. Tourists spinning round and round. I search the crevices between the marquees, spotting an Irish pub Tag loved. The corner where we saw Mikhail Baryshnikov buy a newspaper in the rain. The tiny window above the bodega where a seamstress performs miracles for actresses who are melting away.

The last time I heard Tag's voice was nine months ago. I was alone in my apartment and he was alone in his loft. It was three o'clock in the morning when he called, asking about my neighborhood sounds. His voice soothed me and I was drifting in and out. We fell asleep that way sometimes, two voices on two phones propped up on pillows, ninety blocks between us.

That night, we were quiet for a long time. I was on the edge of a dream. Then Tag's voice, soft as breath, whispered, "I can't bear it anymore."

Something in the edge of his voice startled me wide awake and the phone slipped off my ear. I grabbed for it and it slipped again. When I got it back, I held on as tightly as I could and spoke his name into the receiver but he was gone. I called back. He didn't pick up. I threw on my clothes, ran for the door, and as my cab sliced through the length of Manhattan, I must have known, the same way I do now. The finality hanging in the air, thick as fog.

So many walls I've erected in my mind, so many spaces I've worked hard to wash clean.

I will not remember our parents' death.

I will not remember Tag's lifeless body.

But I cannot forget the down of fine hair on his chest and legs, the way it tickled my skin as we moved together in the dark. I cannot forget the smell of him, the taste of him, so strange and so familiar. That, I cannot forget.

I've carried the key to Tag's loft in my pocket every day for nine months. When I step inside, there is the lingering scent of a sandal wood candle; the white walls, pristinely clean; the real estate cards stacked on the kitchen counter; the overhead lights sparkling against polished concrete floors.

I bristle thinking of the estate lawyers' thrill when the reluctant twin no longer stands in their way to such a profitable sale.

When I get to the bathroom, I'm not afraid the way I thought I might be. I crack open the small, high window above the toilet, run my hands over the porcelain tub. It is white. So very white.

Where Tag last stood, last breathed.

I take off my shoes, my scuffed nylons, skirt, sweater, panties, bra.

I draw the bath scalding hot but slide in without flinching. As I sink down, I think of the woman standing on the curb, her lover in some brownstone or penthouse uptown. Untouchable.

My skin pinkens as I look up toward the window and listen.

Music. The clinking of glasses. Laughter.

The city is alive. It flows like a river.

PHOTOS WITH SAMPA CLODDS

RAE ROZMAN

FULL FATHOM

open doors and windows that let the flies and entropy in jackson
pollock swirls painted so it looks like an accident what is intent but
the blending of blues and greens marble rolling across polished
linoleum we are small small small fit on a glass bauble small and
how do we not feel when the world is spinning tilted off axis have
you found the steady center of the universe in cans of acrylic paint
and thick bristle brushes have you found the breath somewhere
below all the layers

POETRY

RAE ROZMAN

VIEWS FROM THE INSIDE

Breath.
Night spread deep and willing/who is the dream the memory the
nightmare/dragon spiraling towards the sky/claws outstretched/
open maw sharp teeth/filed on splinters/tang of metallic blood

Breath.
A rush the dark the wind in your hair what is power but the
snapping jaws of predation close around confidence shake the lava
lamp wax bubbles rising rising rising

Breath.
Supernova. The world splits open. Fire. Inexplicable   chasms.
The interstices between stars. Between talons. Leave the sky.
Negative space.

Stop.

MATTHEW CHAMBERLIN

THE MAGIC CLOAK

WITH THE BIG RACE LOOMING, my anxiety got so bad I went to see my old fourth grade teacher Ms. Jane, who'd quit teaching for the motivational therapy business.

"What exactly is motivational therapy, Ms. Jane?" We sat on the balcony of her new apartment overlooking the park because everywhere else was filled with moving boxes.

"That's Doctor Jane these days, Robbie. Anyway, most therapy proceeds cautiously through incremental advances whereas I focus on short term goals where a quick fix is beneficial, like this competition of yours." She studied me a moment. "To be honest, I'm surprised you'd take part in a footrace. I don't remember you being gifted athletically."

"That hasn't changed," I admitted. It was Sara Q. who'd decided that my onetime friend James and I would run through the park, to determine which of us would be her lover until the end of time.

"My gosh, little Sara? What's James up to these days?"

"He landlords properties in the art district."

Dr. Jane frowned. "There's been a spate of evictions recently. Artists are being forced out into the cold, including friends of mine."

"That's James, all right. He wants to upscale his buildings which he says will pave the way for real progress, economically speaking."

"Progress for who, I wonder?"

"Good question, Dr. Jane."

She opened a legal pad. "Let's begin, Robbie. What are your deepest fears and insecurities, and to what extent can we attribute them to parental overindulgence or childhood spankings, bed wettings, silent treatments, et cetera?"

The silent treatment wasn't part of my parents' disciplinary repertoire but it had been an effective tool of Dr. Jane's back in the fourth grade. "That's easy, Dr. Jane. Being alone has always terrified me."

"Why so?"

"It goes back to a trip to the art museum when I was nine. I wandered into an exhibit of papier-mâché trees and I guess I had a reaction to the chemicals. Somehow, I got the idea I'd been abandoned in a real forest."

"Wait a minute, Robbie. Wasn't that our class trip in the fourth grade?" Her expression grew thoughtful. "I recall that you climbed one of the trees and did considerable damage. The artist was furious. We were banned from the museum until the end of time."

"It was the fumes, Dr. Jane," I explained.

"Mm-hm." Dr. Jane jotted down a few notes. "We need to speed things up here, Robbie. Let's go inside and try some old-fashioned therapies."

Once we'd squeezed in between the boxes, Dr. Jane handed me a pair of box-cutters. "Imagine there's an invisible cloak hidden in one of these boxes, Robbie. When you find it and put it on, a new you will awaken, one who lacks the frailties and timidity of the real you."

Intrigued, I began slicing experimentally. As the cardboard parted, each box gave a small, satisfying exhalation. Soon time was passing without me really noticing it.

After a half hour all I'd found was Dr. Jane's old teaching dresses and a hoard of unsorted origami sculptures, mostly small woodland animals that crumbled at a touch.

"Robbie, how about some cocoa?" She was transferring the dresses I unpacked to closets and a bureau that had emerged.

"Yes, please."

As we sat sipping cocoa I asked after Dr. Jane's husband, who'd been an artist of one stripe or another at the nearby community college, if memory served.

"Paul could live on the moon for all I care, Robbie. I imagine he feels the same about me, or so I was led to believe when he started sleeping with his students."

"That's terrible, Dr. Jane."

"I thought so too, but it didn't stop him from running off with Elspeth, if that's really a name people are given." She nodded at a potted plant I hadn't noticed before. "That's one of his best pieces."

It wasn't a plant at all, I saw, but a concretion of paste and pulp. Papier-mâché! "Say, did your ex-husband know the artist from the museum we visited—the one whose tree I climbed?"

"That was Paul." Dr. Jane's tone was bleak. "It was his tree you mauled. That was the beginning of the end for us, more or less."

"Oh, no, Dr. Jane."

She sighed and patted the floor. "What's done is done, Robbie. I did okay in the divorce. Come over by me, and let's try some lucid dreaming."

I lay back with my eyes closed.

"You can *Om*, if you like," Dr. Jane instructed. "Good grief, not so loud. Imagine you're a wood-nymph or a forest elf—a pliant creature who's receptive to external forces."

"That sounds like me already, Dr. Jane."

"Hmph. Now, explore your dreamworld in a carefree fashion, but watch out for hidden dangers, trap floors, and boogeymen and so forth."

Soon, I was traipsing through a succession of garden-variety anxiety dreams with fresh purpose, reshaping each one according to a more pleasing narrative in which destiny rose to greet me with outspread arms. It was working, I thought. And yet; and yet.

"You're weeping," observed Dr. Jane. "Try to suspend any sentimentality such as regret or shame, desire, et cetera."

"Sorry. I dreamt I was back in that papier-mâché forest all over again."

"For crying out loud, Robbie. That was thirty-eight years ago."

Dr. Jane lit a cigarette and I coughed until my eyes were streaming. Gritting her teeth, she ground the butt into the soil of the potted plant. It promptly caught fire. "Jesus!" She threw her cocoa on the blaze, which gave a long, wet hiss.

For a moment she gazed at the ruined plant, then tucked it under one arm and strolled out to the balcony, dropping it over the edge. Returning, she slumped in a chair, her expression unreadable.

"Sorry, Dr. Jane."

She made an indeterminate gesture. It seemed like a good idea to call it a day, so I suggested we pick up where we'd left off in the morning.

That evening I facetimed with Sara. She took the call in bed, the soft pile of her hair fanned out behind her. "Robin! You were supposed to call hours ago." She seemed distracted, her bosom heaving as though she was recovering from some gentle exertion. Also, Robin was her sister.

"It's me, darling. Robbie. Are you okay?"

"Oh. Robbie. I might have a cold, actually." Something happened offscreen and she issued a small sound.

"Should I come over? I'll make some cocoa."

"Now's not good. What did you want, Robbie?"

"I have great news. Dr. Jane's helping me prepare for the race."

"You mean Ms. Jane from the fourth grade? She must be in her eighties."

"Eighty-one. It's working really well, I'm super motivated already."

"That's cheating," said a voice. The screen darkened suddenly, as if covered by a pillow.

"Sara?" I asked. "Who was that?"

"I'm losing the call, Robbie. Must be a bad connection."

"But I wanted to share more about my meeting with Dr. Jane."

"Maybe you and she should move in together," Sara suggested.

The line went dead and she didn't answer when I called back. I guess the connection had gone really bad.

The next day, Dr. Jane started us off with some stretching exercises. She seemed concerned by my lack of flexibility. "You're nearly fifty, Robbie. It's time you took better care of yourself."

"You're right, Dr. Jane." Gamely trying to hug one knee, I told her about my call with Sara.

Dr. Jane grimaced. "Poor Robbie. If I had to guess, I'd say James was making love to Sara while you were facetiming."

"Ha, ha. That's crazy." I looked away; the day was brighter than I realized. Sunlight streamed through the windows and entered my brain in a hot, white flood.

Dr. Jane tried various strategies to get me out of my melancholy, igniting incense and perforating my skin with floppy needles. "This'll realign your energy flow," she explained.

"Ouch. That hurts. Can I open more boxes, instead?"

She plucked out the needles, flapping a hand dismissively toward the box cutters.

This time I tried to visualize the magic cloak as I worked. Because it was invisible, what came to mind was a weightless garment made of thousands of translucent scales, which somehow redirected or warped light.

Soon, my mood was improving. I'd been too down on myself lately. That was no way to go into a big race; anyway, it wasn't so crazy to think I might win this thing! "Say, Dr. Jane. What do you think about my chances tomorrow?"

She was thumbing through a magazine. "Wasn't James a track and field star?"

That's right, he competed all through college. He must have a wall of trophies.

With a poof, my motivational progress reversed itself.

"Easy does it with those box cutters, hon."

Watching the sunset from her balcony, Dr. Jane tried to pep me up one last time. "Maybe think about re-channeling your creative energy, Robbie. Origami can help. Do you remember when we made ducks and rabbits in the fourth grade?"

"I guess so. Thanks for the idea, Dr. Jane."

It was a pleasant evening, but I was alarmed to see dots of orange light flicker to life in the park below. The pungent aroma of wood smoke wafted up. "Dr. Jane, the park's on fire!"

She laughed, going on to explain that the homeless artists were sleeping in whatever green spaces they could find. The nights were getting chilly; those were their campfires.

The next day I got to the park around five in the afternoon. Everything was green and immaculate except for the colonies of homeless artists. Instead of unhappy or desperate, though, they looked relaxed and even contemplative, which somehow depressed me more.

One older couple was assembling some kind of public art installation, dipping cardboard in a powerful-smelling solvent then wrapping the soggy material around a tall frame. I sensed they were the real deal: professional artists who were entirely capable of transforming the ugly reality of homelessness into something true and transcendent.

Passing the duck pond, I dodged the ducks as they lunged their sinuous necks through the barrier and snapped like angry dogs. Sara and James waited by the swings. Just before they noticed me, I ducked behind a sprawling hydrangea and shut my eyes tightly. I lucid dreamed that I had the magic cloak and could walk right up to them, completely invisible.

In my dream, they didn't have a clue. Sara gazed around tiredly, like she usually did when we were together. James complained about the homeless artists which he should have thought of before he'd evicted them all. He leaned towards Sara. "Do you think Robbie knew I was under the covers while you two were facetiming?"

I wrenched myself awake; Dr. Jane's techniques were too potent for casual use. "Here I am," I called, my voice more shrill than I'd intended. "How many laps are we running? James, I should get a head start because of your background in track and field," I suggested.

"Never mind all that," said Sara. "Ready?" There was a sharp clap from a little pistol she held. "Go."

James sprinted off but my shoelace was undone. "Wait, I need a do-over."

Sara was climbing onto the swings, a distant expression on her face.

"James," I called.

He extended a middle finger while jogging backwards in a cocky way. A duck stuck its neck out, pecked him on the rear, and James gave a little shriek. Annoyed, he sped away. I couldn't catch him if I tried. Now, Sara was really swinging. She leaned into a series of steep, plunging arcs.

"Darling," I cried. "You're going too high." I hated how plaintive I sounded. Suddenly, I felt something give—my shoelace had snapped. I had to get away. Casting around, I saw some peaceful fir trees in the distance and ran for them.

The wind sprang up and a few dark clouds chased each other across the sky. The sunshine was a warm gold. I wandered among the trees, catching sight of Dr. Jane's building now and again. A creek gurgled invitingly but I thought better of drinking downstream from those artist encampments.

I came out of the woods to find I'd arrived back where the older artist couple was working. They had nearly finished their sculpture, a life-sized papier-mâché tree with long, tapering branches and a canopy made of thousands of paper leaves.

"Hello," I said. "What a gorgeous tree."

The man nodded uninterestedly but then snapped into alertness. "Hands off the artwork. Yes, you. You can't climb here. Stop him, Elspeth!"

I scampered up the tree into the cool shade of the canopy. All around the leaves shimmered in a lovely way.

"Are you okay up there? Would you like some water or a fruit bar?" Elspeth shaded her eyes with one hand.

"Don't make him feel *welcome*," the man hissed.

"Oh, Paul."

They argued but stopped at the sound of someone approaching.

"Hi there," said a familiar voice. "I'm in the market for some classy outdoor art for a building I own downtown." Looking around at all the fake plants everywhere, James said, "You know? I can't stand these fake plants everywhere."

"It's not for sale," Elspeth explained. "We're protesting the unfair evictions. Each leaf represents a homeless artist."

"Well, not yet, anyway," said Paul.

James was in his running gear. "That's cool. Hey, is someone up there?"

Paul waved angrily. "We've got an uninvited guest."

"A squatter, huh?" James chuckled. "That's a problem I'm quite familiar with. We could smoke him out, if you want."

Paul hesitated. "Let's try it."

"What? No." Elspeth was horrified.

They dipped a piece of carboard in the solvent and James produced a lighter. Acrid smoke billowed up. I coughed and choked, desperate to breathe. Tearing off a branch, I fanned the air.

"He's messing up your protest tree, man," said James.

Paul gave a shout of outrage. I felt funny, like clinging to a single balloon. Luckily Dr. Jane had taught me to self-soothe. I pulled off a leaf and folded it into a little rabbit, then tore off another leaf and folded that one into a duck. Again and again I folded up little forest creatures and let them drift to the grass below.

Elspeth picked up a paper chipmunk. "Paul? He's making origami with the leaves."

Paul kicked the tree, wild with fury. "It's happening again. Get out of my tree, you son of a bitch."

James joined in, kicking and laughing. I think he knew it was me up there.

"Out, out, out," screamed Paul.

James delivered a gleeful flying karate kick and the tree lurched. Elspeth covered her face.

"Wait," Paul gasped as the tree tilted. "Stop kicking!"

The papier-mâché cushioned the fall. I lay in the wreckage for a while, just relieved to breathe fresh air.

Peeking through tangled branches, James giggled and flipped me off again. "Loser," he said. "I need something a little stronger for my building," he mentioned to Paul then sauntered off.

Elspeth gave me a bottle of water. "Are you okay?" She took Paul's arm. It was dusk. Dull-eyed, he let himself be led away.

After a while I made myself get up, stepping carefully on shaky legs. In the distance came a yelp—Paul and Elspeth were walking past the duck pond.

I hadn't gone far when some homeless artists waved me over to their campfire.

"Pull up a seat, man."

"Thank you." I collapsed criss-cross-applesauce. The artists were watching the embers in a companionable silence. Maybe they thought I was a homeless artist too.

The fire waned. "Anybody got any kindling?" someone asked.

I was glad for the chance to help. "I know where there's some." Heading back to the wreckage, I gathered some big pieces of Paul's papier-mâché tree.

There was scattered applause when they saw me returning. "Plenty more where this came from," I said proudly, dumping the branches on the coals.

Whoosh.

I'd forgotten about the solvent. As the fireball subsided, the artists rolled around patting at the flames. "Oh, jeez," I said. "Oh, man."

Nobody seemed badly hurt. A middle aged woman in paint-spattered overalls leaned toward the flames, an unlit cigarette in her lips. She screwed her eyes shut. "Do it again."

The laughter lasted a while. Feeling better, I pulled a leaf from my pocket. It seemed like a good time for some origami.

"What's that, hon?" someone asked.

I held the paper rabbit up, but too close to the fire. It burst into flame. For a second I juggled it in my cupped hands. As it burned away to nothing, the artists *oohed* and *aahed*.

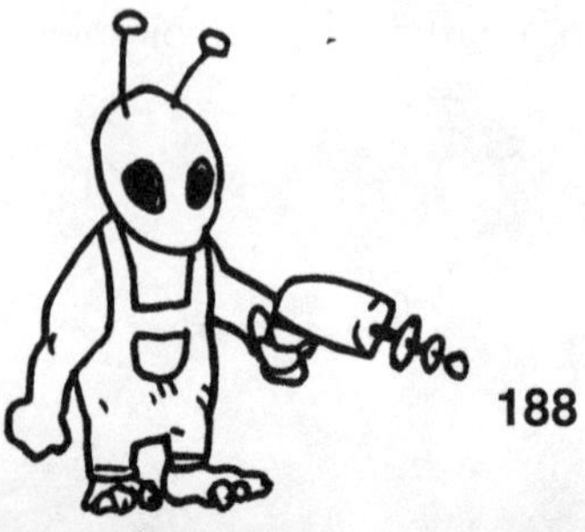

CONTRIBUTORS' BIOS

CONSTANCE BACCHUS currently lives with her daughter in the Columbia Basin of Washington state. Her poetry can be found in or forthcoming in various literary journals including *Cirque Journal, DreichBroad Review, Permafrost, Blue River Review* and *Salmon Creek Journal.* Her newest book is DIVORCING FLOWERS (Alien Buddha Press, 2021) although she does have others including SECRET DAMTHINGS.

MATTHEW CHAMBERLIN's short stories and poetry have appeared in *A-minor, Typehouse Literary Magazine, Jersey Devil Press, Gone Lawn,* among other places; and he has been nominated for a Pushcart prize. He lives and writes in Virginia, where he directs the Independent Scholars major at James Madison University.

FRANKLIN K.R CLINE is the author of SO WHAT (VA-11) and THE BEATLES' SECOND ALBUM (VA-86), both available via Vegetarian Alcoholic Press. He is an enrolled member of the Cherokee Nation who lives in Kansas City, Missouri, with Six and Olivia.

MARISA CRANE is a writer, jock, and sweatpants enthusiast. Their work has appeared or is forthcoming in *Joyland, No Tokens, TriQuarterly, Passages North, Florida Review, Catapult, Lit Hub, The Rumpus,* and elsewhere. Their debut novel, I KEEP MY EXOSKELETONS TO MYSELF, will be released on January 17, 2023. You can pre-order it through PenguinRandomhouse.com.

SHAWN DELGADO is the author of the chapbook A SKY HALF-DISMANTLED and his poems have appeared in *The Birmingham Poetry Review, The Courtland Review, Five Points, The Greensboro Review, Terminus Magazine,* and elsewhere. He lives in Greensboro with his cats, books, and frisbees where he currently teaches poetry workshops at the University of North Carolina at Greensboro and Guilford College.

CONTRIBUTORS' BIOS, PART II

ZAKIYYAH DZUKOGI is a 17-year-old Nigerian poet. She is the author of Carved (a poetry collection); winner of the Nigeria Prize for Teen Authors 2021, a prize she had earlier won the second-place position in 2020. She is a winner of Brigitte Poirson Poetry Prize 2021 as well as the Splendors of Dawn Poetry Prize 2019. Her works have been published or are forthcoming in *Melbourne Culture Corner, Olney Magazine, rigorous, The Account, mixed mag, the beatnik cowboy, Kalahari, spillwords, Sledgehammer, the Dillydoun review, Tilted House*, and others.

DANIEL GALEF has been an actor, a teacher, a door-to-door poll taker, and a dictionary definition (Merriam-Webster, "interfaculty," adj.[2]), but currently he is a graduate instructor of English at Florida State University and Associate Poetry Editor of *Able Muse.* His short fiction has appeared in *Juked, the American Bystander, Bewildering Stories*, and the 2020 Best Small Fictions anthology. He also writes poems and plays. Galef lives behind an Aldi in the Florida Panhandle where he bicycles through haunted swamps, collects counterfeit coins, and has not had a shave or a haircut in four years.

BERNADETTE GEYER is the author of The Scabbard of Her Throat (The Word Works) and editor of My Cruel Invention: A Contemporary Poetry Anthology (Meerkat Press). Her writings and translations have appeared in *Barrow Street, Fourteen Hills, The Massachusetts Review,* and elsewhere. Geyer works as a writer, editor, and translator in Berlin, Germany.

ROBIN GOW is a trans poet and young adult author. They are the author of Our Lady of Perpetual Degeneracy (Tolsun Books 2020) and the chapbook Honeysuckle (Finishing Line Press 2019). Their first young adult novel, A Million Quiet Revolutions is slated for publication winter 2022 with FSG. Gow's poetry has recently been published in *POETRY, New Delta Review,* and *Washington Square Review.*

CONTRIBUTORS' BIOS, EPISODE 3

GRETA HAYER received her MFA at the University of New Orleans and has work appearing in *Beneath Ceaseless Skies, Cossmass Infinites, Booth, Maudlin House*, and *Flint Hills Review*. She received a bachelor's degree in history from the College of Wooster, where she studied fairy tales and medieval medicine. Her column, "In Search of the Dream World," can be found at *Luna Station Quarterly*. She lives in New Orleans with her husband and their three alien cats.

SORAMIMI HANAREJIMA is the neuropunk author of Literary Devices for Coping and whose recent work can be found in *Moss, Vestal Review*, and *Lunch Ticket*.

REBECCA HIGGINS is a writer based in Minnesota. When she's not writing, she edits children's nonfiction books. Her work has appeared in *Fatal Flaw, Trailer Park Quarterly*, and *The Fulcrum*, among other places. Rebecca knows firsthand what it's like to experience mental illness and encourages everyone to practice self-love, and maybe get a cat.

CLAIRE HOPPLE is the author of four books. Her fiction has appeared in *Hobart, Vol. 1 Brooklyn, The Rupture, New World Writing*, and others. She's just a steel town girl on a Saturday night. More at clairehopple.com.

SATOSHI IWAI was born and lives in Kanagawa, Japan. He writes poems in English and in Japanese. His English work has appeared in *Heavy Feather Review, FLAPPERHOUSE, Small Po[r]tions, Your Impossible Voice, Poetry Is Dead*, and elsewhere.

CASEY McCONAHAY's work has appeared in *December, Lake Effect*, and *Southern Humanities Review*. He lives in northwest Ohio.

CONTRIBUTORS' BIOS, TBD4

GARY GLASS wrote his first novel over monsoon season in the Himalayas. He has been working for several years on his fifth novel, a mad monstrosity of a book called The Swan of Antares. He has also been an ad writer in Taiwan, a racehorse exerciser in Japan, a registered nurse in Indiana, and has a software engineering patent. He created and ran for ten years a social networking site for readers and writers called BookBalloon. He currently lives with his wife in Valencia, Spain.

After years of caring for wolves in a remote mountain sanctuary, **LAURA McGEHEE** is pursuing her MFA in fiction at the University of Virginia, where she can be found embracing the trappings of modernity and/or rejecting the stain of man's hand. Lately, this means running not to exercise, but to exorcise (demons). With her own stained hands, she writes about eros and isolation, so that you do not have to. Though of course, she welcomes the company. She is playing it cool. Please never leave. Her short-form work has been featured in *Cactus Heart*, *Gertrude Press*, *Spider Road Press*, and *Sinister Wisdom*.

LINCOLN MICHEL's debut novel The Body Scout (Orbit) was named one of the ten best SFF books of 2021 by The New York Times. He is also the author of the story collection Upright Beasts (Coffee House Press) and the co-editor of the anthologies Tiny Crimes (Catapult) and Tiny Nightmares (Catapult). His fiction appears in *The Paris Review*, *Granta*, *F&SF*, *NOON*, *Lightspeed*, the Pushcart Prize anthology, and elsewhere. You can find him online at lincolnmichel.com and @thelincoln.

KYLE E MILLER is a naturalist and writer living in Michigan. He can usually be found in the dunes or forests, turning up logs looking for life. Past incarnations include zookeeper, video game critic, retail manager, stablehand, and writing tutor. His work has appeared in *Clarkesworld*, *Breath & Shadow*, and *Thoreau on Mackinac*. You can find more at kyle-e-miller.com.

MICHAEL P. MORAN is a nonfiction and fiction writer from Long Island, New York. His creative nonfiction works were published in *The Chaffin Journal*, *Miracle Monocle*, *Emerald City*, *The Bookends Review*, and *Please See Me*. He is currently working on two projects: a collection of essays centered on his life with type 1 diabetes and a novel both beautiful and terrifying. His wife encourages his typewriter to sing, and his child wants to know when someone will publish his chapter book about the bird. He can be reached on Instagram @mikesgotaremington.

MARY LYNN REED's fiction has appeared, or will soon appear, in *Fourteen Hills*, *Colorado Review*, *Mississippi Review*, *Free State Review*, and many other places. She has an MFA in Creative Writing from the University of Maryland. She lives in western New York with her wife, and together they co-edit the online literary journal *MoonPark Review*.

XAVIER REYNA is a poet from the Rio Grande Valley.

JOHN RIEBOW was born and raised in Philadelphia, where he attended the W. B. School High School of Agriculture Sciences. He holds a Bachelor of Science degree in Landscape Architecture from Temple University, is an LEED-Accredited Professional, and serves as Director of Design for a design-build-development general contractor. His work has been featured in *Abandoned Towers*, *Adelaide*, *Audience*, *Aurora Wolf*, *The Bethany Reader*, *The Chaffey Review*, *Down the Rabbit Hole*, *Dual Coast*, *Ensorcelled*, *Forge Journal*, *Freedom Fiction Journal*, *Gold Dust*, *Hope Screams Eternal*, *Killing the Angel*, *The Loch Raven Review*, *Mulberry Fork Review*, *Ninth Aspect*, and *Scarlet Leaf Review*. He has been writing fiction, poetry and radio drama scripts for over twenty years and is currently working on a novel and a collection of short fiction.

CONTRIBUTORS' BIOS, FINALE

MICHELLE ROSS is the author of the story collections THERE'S SO MUCH THEY HAVEN'T TOLD YOU, winner of the 2016 Moon City Short Fiction Award, and SHAPESHIFTING, winner of the 2020 Stillhouse Press Short Fiction Award (and forthcoming in 2021). Her fiction has appeared in *Alaska Quarterly Review, Colorado Review, Electric Literature, Witness,* and other venues. Her work is included in BEST SMALL FICTIONS 2021, BEST MICROFICTIONS 2021 and 2020, the WIGLEAF Top 50 2019, and other anthologies. She is fiction editor of *Atticus Review.* michellenross.com

TOM ROTH earned an MFA from Chatham University. His most recent publications are in *Grattan Street Press* and *Great Lakes Review.* He has a publication forthcoming in *Talking River Review.* He teaches freshman composition at Chatham University. He also tutors for Pittsburgh Montessori School.

RAE ROZMAN (she/her) is a middle school educator who occasionally moonlights as a poet. When not gushing about books to her students, she can be found playing board games or eating vegan cupcakes. She lives in Ohio with her partner and their two adorable rescue bunnies.

BILLY THRASHER is a graduate of the MFA program at Lindenwood University. He writes at home, at the coffee shop, at the park, and in his car during lunch breaks. He has written works in *Moon Magazine, Lagom: A Journal, Jenny, Dovecote, Panoplyzine, White Wall, As You Were: The Military Review,* and *Dunes Review.*

SAMUEL ZAGULA is an anxious and broken person born in 1996. He currently publishes a small magazine of stories and drawings made solely by himself titled *Addicts Idiots And Losers*, with a new issue released every three weeks. He graduated from Colorado College with a BA in Philosophy and spends too much time alone in his room. You can find him at addictsidiotsandlosers.com.

DID YOU MISS THESE OTHER FINE TITLES?

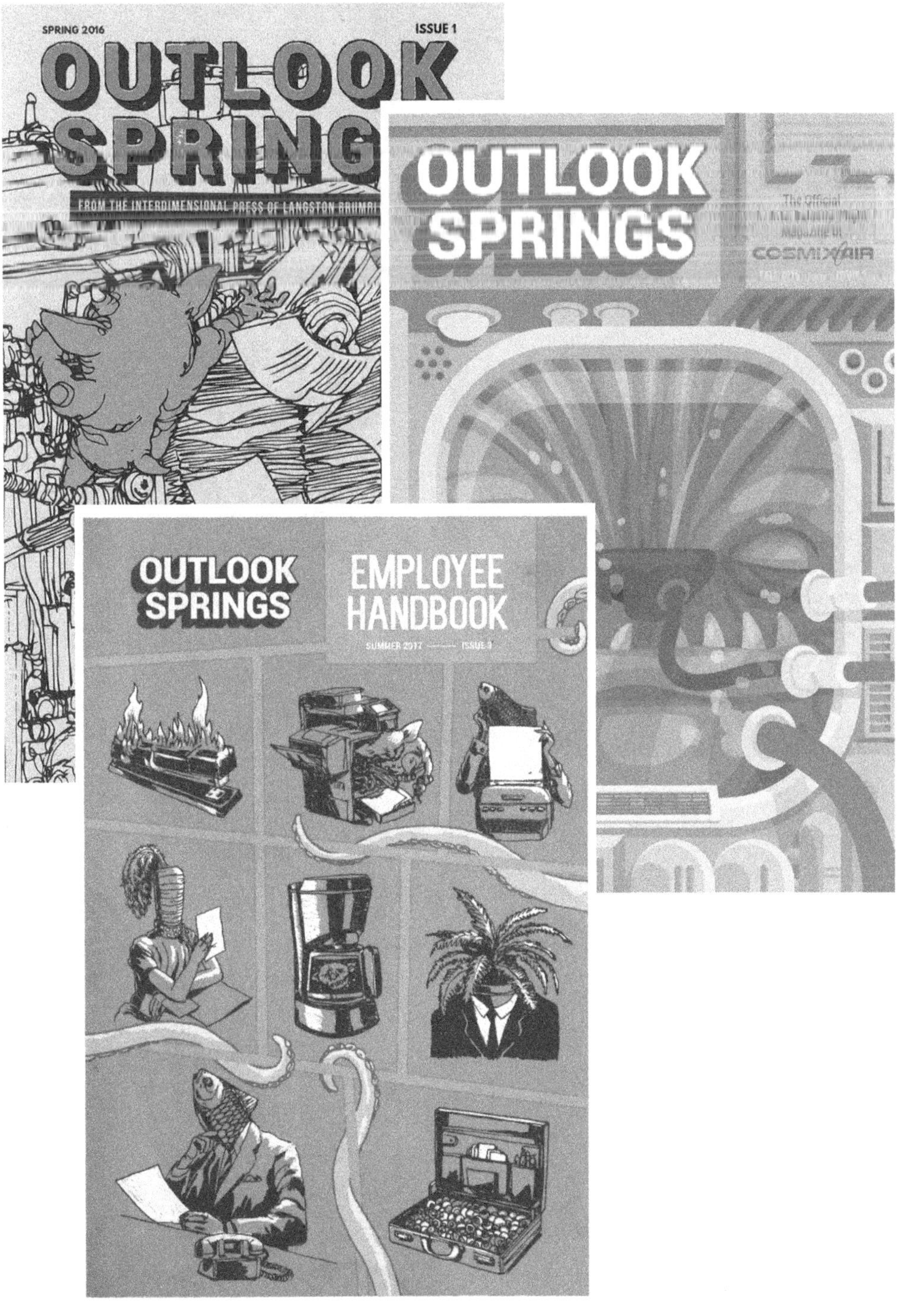

SPRING 2016
ISSUE 1
OUTLOOK SPRINGS

OUTLOOK SPRINGS

OUTLOOK SPRINGS
EMPLOYEE HANDBOOK

DID YOU MISS THESE OTHER FINE TITLES?

THE PARKIEST PARK IN OUTLOOK SPRINGS

OUTLOOK SPRIN

INTERDIMENSIONAL P

EST. 3782 ISSUE #4

FRESH AIR
'91

The Official Yearbook of
OUTLOOK
SPRINGS
ACADEMY

(OUTLOOK SPR-
INGS ISSUE 5)

DID YOU MISS THESE OTHER FINE TITLES?

Nº 6

OUTLOOK SPRINGS
MANOR & ESTATE

OFFICIAL TOUR BOO

CAMP SUMMER

OUTLOOK SPRINGS' ONLY SUMMER-TIME CAMP

IT'S ALWAYS
SUMMER HERE

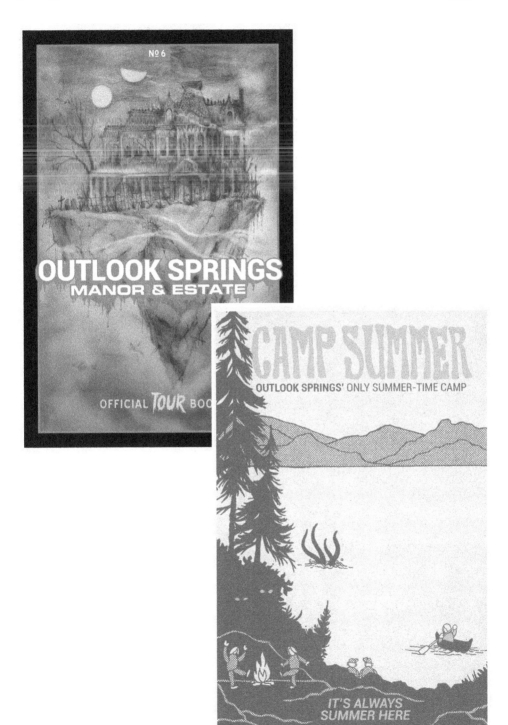